The Squirrel Chronicles

Book One

by Ron Ostlund

PublishAmerica
Baltimore

© 2006 by Ron Ostlund.
All rights reserved. No part of this book may be reproduced, stored in a retrieval system or transmitted in any form or by any means without the prior written permission of the publishers, except by a reviewer who may quote brief passages in a review to be printed in a newspaper, magazine or journal.

First printing

All characters appearing in this work are fictitious. Any resemblance to real persons, living or dead, is purely coincidental.

At the specific preference of the author, PublishAmerica allowed this work to remain exactly as the author intended, verbatim, without editorial input.

ISBN: 1-4241-2651-7
PUBLISHED BY PUBLISHAMERICA, LLLP
www.publishamerica.com
Baltimore

Printed in the United States of America

To my wife Sue who has read more squirrel stories than required in the phrase, "For better or for worse."

List of Stories

The Great Seed Heist 7

An Alternate Plan 23

A Plan Revised 35

A Change of Plans 52

A Plan Reversed 72

A Field of Seeds 90

The Eye of the Beholder 103

The Attack of the Mutant Squirrels 123

Oh, Oh, Penny Sue 141

It's Not Always About the Seeds 159

The Seed Maker 174

Hostage Situation 192

The Society of Ben Hog 207

CHAPTER 1

The Great Seed Heist

"I've got to hand it to you Roscoe, this is the best idea you've ever had." Jules had just come from the squirrel feeder. He'd done his part, eating as many seeds as he could and was lying with his back against a tree root, fighting to stay awake.

Roscoe, the one he was talking to, listened but kept an eye on the feeder. "Where's Marvin? He was supposed to…never mind I see him."

He watched Marvin dart between two trees, press himself against a fence post, sprint across the yard and pull up close to the deck rail.

"Marvin, for gosh sakes just go to the feeder, there's no need for the cloak and dagger stuff." As he spoke he waved an arm indicating Marvin should get on with the business of emptying the feeder.

Marvin did his job, polishing off the last inch of seeds that remained at the bottom of the feeder tube. When he finished he hopped down, ran across the yard and took his place next to Roscoe.

"Why don't you just take out an advertisement in the *Abner Echo* and let the whole world know where we are?" Roscoe shook his head, bewildered. He'd gone over the plan with the seed heist team several times but now that he was about to kick the project off they were wandering around like a bunch of blind squirrels hunting for an acorn. He heard slow, regular breathing coming from Jules and knew he'd be one squirrel short for the second phase of the operation.

At least he had Marvin with him, he figured the two of them could handle the next part without additional help.

His idea for the seed heist was based on a question he'd asked himself many times; why fiddle around with a tube of seeds when you can have the whole bag? When he finished going over his plan with the team he'd convinced them if they were successful there'd be a continuous supply of seeds within easy reach. They'd no longer have to leave their nests to get something to eat on bitterly cold mornings or when an early rain made the ground so muddy you had to hunt for a dry place to land. When his plan was complete they'd simply turn to a large bag propped in the corner of their nest, help themselves to a handful of seeds and roll back over in their warm beds.

His plan, however, was not without detractors. "Give it up Roscoe," Edgar Chairman of The Committee to Protect Neighborhood Resources told him when he heard what he was up to. "Things aren't so bad the way they are. Besides, it doesn't hurt to get a little exercise before breakfast. Especially someone your age, burn off some of that youthful energy." Then he added in solemn tones, "If you go through with this crazy plan of yours, you're going to mess things up for all of us."

Roscoe was not going to allow a few fair weather squirrels to change his mind. *Operation Seed Heist* would go forward, with or without the Committee's approval.

He and Marvin were hidden from the house by a tree branch that dipped close to the ground at the back of the yard. From their position they could see anything that moved in front of them. He knew this part could take awhile so he gestured for Marvin to relax and for the first time in a couple of hours allowed himself to do the same.

He'd had the idea for some time but in his usual patient way of going about things, he'd waited for the right moment.

"What's going on now?" Marvin was picking at a seed caught between his teeth while he scratched his back against the tree trunk.

"Surveillance, Marvin. It's called surveillance." Roscoe let out a heavy sigh. "We talked about this at our last meeting, remember?" For the first time he wondered if he had chosen the right one to be his second in command.

"Should I be doing something while I surveil? Or, whatever it was you said we were doing." Marvin is a squirrel of action, sitting around, staring at the back of a house is not his idea of getting something done.

"It means we wait and watch Marvin. That's the hardest part of any oper…hold on, look over by the garage door. I thought I saw something move."

Marvin leaned forward, straining to see what Roscoe was talking about. "Okay, okay. Got it." He spoke quickly, "I see him." He patted Roscoe on the back.

"Start counting Marvin. I need to know how long it takes from the time he comes around the corner of the garage until he gets to the feeder." Roscoe was looking at his list of action items.

"Oh right. Sorry, I forgot. A thousand one, a thousand…" Marvin started counting.

"To yourself, Marvin. Please, count quietly to yourself."

Roscoe checked on the one they call Seed Man because he was the one who filled the feeder when it was empty. He was carrying a sack the size of a large grocery bag across the yard.

"Sure Roscoe," Marvin paused a little embarrassed. "A thou…uh, where was I?"

"A thousand five. You were at a thousand five." Roscoe snapped out the answer while he made a few calculations in the dirt. Out of the corner of his eye he could see Marvin's lips move as he counted. He got back to the task at hand, trying to determine how many Community members he needed for the seed bag team. "The average squirrel can lift, say, a half a pound? No that's expecting too much. How about a fourth of a pound? The sack Seed Man is carrying looks like it weighs five or six pounds. I'll say six to be on the safe side. That would be," he drew a line under the numbers he'd written in the dirt. He looked in the air then studied his paw. "Twenty-four squirrels to carry the bag from the feeder to the staging area."

He sighed. "That's not going to cut it. Twenty-four squirrels trying to carry one sack? They'll be tripping over each other and never get it away in time."

He reluctantly came to the conclusion that he had to buy some time for the seed bag team and to do that he was going to need help.

Roscoe never felt comfortable leaving his Neighborhood where he knew the location of each limb on every tree. There, he can move from place to place without having to think about where to jump next or which yards are occupied by mean dogs.

Leaving made him edgy; there were too many things that could go wrong. For one thing, squirrels in other Neighborhoods weren't all that friendly to outsiders and for another most dogs saw him as a quick, between meal snack. However, he knew if he wanted to pull off a truly remarkable feat, one they'd be talking about in the Community for years to come he had to face his fears.

Besides, the Edelman Brothers were only two Neighborhoods away and the success or failure of the *Great Seed Heist* might very well rest on their shoulders.

He cautiously made his way through the unfamiliar landscape until he arrived at their front door. He'd never actually met them but he'd heard of their gymnastic exploits from others. They called themselves, *The Flying Edelman Brothers* and even the most adventurous squirrels he'd talked to admitted their acrobatics had to be seen to be believed.

The task facing Roscoe was to share as little of his plan as possible with them while at the same time, convincing them to sign on and be a part of it.

He started to knock on the door in the base of the tree but held up when he heard what sounded like several yips followed by a thud and decided to check it out to see if it spelled danger.

He walked around the tree, saw nothing suspicious and figured every thing was okay so he returned to the door and knocked.

At first there was no response but eventually he heard someone slightly out of breath holler, "It's open. Come in." He pushed on the door, it swung open and he stepped inside.

He blinked trying to make sure he was seeing things correctly or if his eyes hadn't adjusted to the change of moving from bright daylight to the half-light inside. The room he was standing in had no furniture. There were no pictures on the wall or curtains covering the windows and no attempt had been made to cover the dirt floor with rugs or mats.

Starting a few feet above the floor and spaced at varying

distances apart branches, stripped of bark, stretched across the width of the trunk and climbed up the inside of the tree as far as he could see.

He was trying to take all this in and figure out if he'd come to the wrong place when he heard a yip, followed by the sound of something being thrown in the air. There was a soft thud and a thin, muscular squirrel landed in front of him. He wore small gymnastic gloves on his front paws and traces of chalk dust clung to his fur. A gray sleeveless shirt was tucked into a pair of black tights.

"What can I do for you buddy? And you'd better make it quick, my brother Morey hates interruptions when we're working on a new routine."

"Edelman?" Roscoe was having trouble concentrating, he could hear someone swinging on the branches overhead. He'd never seen anything quite like the squirrel standing in front of him or his home gymnasium. "Brothers?" He managed to add. "I'm, ah, looking for them, the Edelmans."

"The Flying Edelmans," the gymnast quickly corrected him. "We've changed or name. It's all legal and everything if that's what you're here about. I'm Rorey by the way in case you're wondering."

"No. No. I'm not here about that. Rorey you say?" Roscoe was beginning to relax, talking seemed to help.

He heard another thud and someone he assumed was Morey, landed gently next to his brother and ended up with his elbow resting on Rorey's shoulder.

"Do we have a problem?" Morey changed positions and smacked his gloved paws together as if he was getting ready to throw Roscoe out. He turned to Rorey and said, "We're loosing valuable time brother. Perfect performance requires perfect practice. You know that and we were far from perfect on the last routine." He gave Roscoe a hard look.

"I'm sorry to disturb your training and I will be as brief as possible but…" Roscoe checked both their faces hoping to see a softening of their features or some sign of interest in what he was about to say. When he failed to see either he continued, "I have a proposition you might be interested in."

"You've got our attention," Rorey looked at his brother, nodded, then back at Roscoe.

It wasn't long before Roscoe had competed a drawing of Seed Man's backyard on the dirt floor. He drew the corner of the garage and the squirrel feeder and made x's between the two locations that followed the path Seed Man normally took to the feeder. He drew more x's and an arrow showing the path the seed bag would take from the time Seed Man set it down to the temporary hiding place at the side of the yard. He wrote out his calculations that showed he would need twenty-four squirrels to carry the bag to safety. He had the team of squirrels on board, he explained, but it will take time for them to move the bag from the feeder to the hiding place. "That's where you come in," he told them as he rubbed his foot over the diagram and erased what he'd drawn.

"Pardon us a second Roscoe." Rorey put his arm around his brother's shoulder and walked with him to the middle of the room.

Roscoe heard mumbling and watched as Rorey made motions with his hand, pointing out to his brother what they could do in terms of a gymnastic routine to buy some time for the seed bag team. His brother responded by shaking his head no, went into a front roll and flipped back up on his feet as if to demonstrate either why his plan wouldn't work or why it would, Roscoe wasn't sure.

The brothers nodded, smacked their paws together and walked back to Roscoe. "We're in," Rorey said with confidence.

"That's great, so let me show you…" Roscoe started to give them directions to his Neighborhood and tell them the time they were supposed to show up but was interrupted by Rorey.

"We'll need some compensation for our performance Roscoe. We are professionals you know." Morey crossed his muscular arms over his chest.

"Compensation?" Roscoe acted like the idea of anyone making a profit off his plan came as a complete surprise to him. "I thought I explained this is just a prank, nobody's getting any, *compensation*, from this little caper." He raised his shoulders and lifted his paws to indicate this was nothing more than a well planned joke.

He even managed a smile and a little laugh when he added, "Nobody's going to get rich off this one guys."

"You're telling us your going to walk away and leave a six pound bag of seeds under a bush?" Morey shook his head. "Excuse me but I don't see that happening."

Rorey leaned forward and clasped his paws together. Morey put his foot in them and after a short, "Yip," Rorey straightened and sent Morey flying upward where he did two complete flips before grabbing a lower bar.

"We've got to get back to work Roscoe and, ah, don't let the door hit you on the way out if you know what I'm saying." With that said Morey reached down, grabbed Rorey's arms and swung him up to the next bar.

They're spectacular, Roscoe thought. Much better than what he'd heard about them. They were perfect for his plan and he couldn't afford to loose them.

"Okay, okay," Roscoe called up to them, "what are we talking about here, seed wise?"

"Half a pound each or it's no deal," Rorey's voice came from high in the tree trunk.

Roscoe did a few, quick calculations. Six pounds take away a pound would leave five pounds for the Community.

"I can live with that," he hollered up to them.

Thud. Thud. Both squirrels lit on their feet, one on either side of Roscoe.

"When did you say this gig was taking place?" Morey asked.

Roscoe gave them the information, they touched paws on the deal and almost immediately the Edelmans leapt in the air and were back working on the rough spots in their new routine.

Roscoe smiled to himself as he walked away from their tree, he'd been prepared to go as high as a pound for each of them if he had to.

His plan was coming together.

The big day arrived and Roscoe moved to the director's position behind the tree limb. It has to happen this morning, he told himself, all the pieces are in place and he sensed it was a onetime opportunity. The Flying Edelmans weren't available the whole day, they had another engagement scheduled for later in the afternoon and he wasn't sure how long he could keep the twenty-four members of the seed bag team gathered by the rose bush under control.

He'd sent Jules and then Marvin out to empty the feeder and they'd returned, somewhat bloated but successful. Jules left to direct the seed bag team while Marvin took his place next to Roscoe, his face was a picture of concentration. He looked at Roscoe, nodded confidently, then turned his gaze to the side of the house.

Roscoe could see the Edelmans stretching and flexing on a tree limb in back of the feeder.

Now it all came down to Seed Man showing up. They'd run this part of the drill three times and each time he'd appeared within minutes of the last seed being taken from the feeder but Roscoe knew in an operation like this there were no guarantees.

The squirrels by the rose bush caught the mood of expectancy and settled down waiting for his signal to move out. The Edelmans removed their warm up jackets and dropped to a lower limb. They looked over and waved a gloved paw to Roscoe indicating they were ready.

Time seemed to slow down. Birds in the vicinity stopped flying and settled in tree limbs at the back of the yard to watch. Even the breeze that had been blowing earlier caught on to what was happening and coasted to a stop choosing to hang around and see how Roscoe's plan would turn out; kites and pinwheels could wait, it wasn't everyday you got to see something like this.

About the time Roscoe was ready to stop the project and write the whole thing off as an idea ahead of it's time he heard the familiar sound of the garage door going up. It meant Seed Man was either running an errand or bringing seeds out to fill the feeder tubes.

Marvin reached over and grabbed Roscoe's arm. When he was sure he had his attention he nodded toward the side of the house. Roscoe looked up and saw Seed Man rounding the corner and heading across the yard toward the feeder carrying a brand new bag of seeds.

Roscoe rose slightly and waved his arms to get the attention of the Flying Edelmans. When he was sure they were looking his way he made a motion with his hand that they should start.

He heard a familiar, "Yip yip," and watched Rorey drop Morey over the limb and grab his front paws.

Seed Man stopped when he saw them hanging upside down

from the tree limb, he was having trouble figuring out what was going on.

The Flying Edelmans began to swing, Rorey's legs were hooked over a limb and he held his brother by the front paws. When they reached the part of the swing that would produce the most momentum, Morey let go and did three somersaults before reaching out and grasping Rorey's paws as he fell toward the ground.

Seed Man couldn't take his eyes off of them. He hollered for someone named Sweetheart to, "Get out here and bring the camera." He knew his friends wouldn't believe what he'd seen unless he could provide some kind of proof.

There was no answer from inside the house.

The Flying Edelmans hung from the limb and with a single, "Yip", Morey swung up and landed on Rorey's shoulders. Both brothers stuck their arms out to the side.

Seed Man hollered for Sweetheart to, "Get a move on it will you, you've got to see this." There was a sense of urgency in his voice; he'd never seen anything like it and he knew it wouldn't last forever.

His second call got the same result as the first, no response. There was a moment when he didn't know what to do but the possibility of catching the performing squirrels on film won out.

He set the bag of seeds on the ground and turned to hurry inside and get his camera.

The success of Roscoe's plan hinged on the one simple act of Seed Man setting the bag down and going inside and it happened.

As soon as Seed Man disappeared around the corner of the garage Roscoe saw the seed bag team leave the rose bush and make a beeline to the seed bag. Under the watchful eye of Jules, they spaced themselves evenly around the bag, each grabbing the side in front of them.

He heard Jules give the command to lift and saw the sack slowly rise off the ground. He heard him give the command to move out and the sack seemed to float above the top of the freshly cut grass as the twenty-four squirrels strained to carry the sack toward the staging area.

Roscoe allowed himself a quick smile. He saw the Flying Edelmans cross the street and head back to their Neighborhood but he knew they'd be back later for their part of the prize.

He checked the side of the garage but saw no sign of Seed Mans return. He looked back and watched the bag continue to sail across the ground toward the staging area where they would temporarily hide it. Once the seed bag was safely hidden and Seed Man had gone back into his house, they would come back and move it to the Clearing.

Things were working exactly the way he'd drawn them on the dirt floor of the Edelman's gymnasium.

He allowed himself a moments satisfaction. He knew from the beginning it was a good plan but with so many things that could go wrong the chance of success was slim. *The Flying Edelmans* could have been late or one of the squirrels on the seed bag team called in sick and the sack would have been too heavy for the others to carry. Edgar and the members of the Committee could have staged a protest at the feeder and blocked the route of the seed bag team.

The sound of squirrels arguing brought him back to the present moment. The bag of seeds was resting at the base of a tree at the edge of the yard. The squirrels on one side insisted they take it around their way while those opposite them pulled and shouted they should go around their side.

The Squirrel Chronicles: Book One

Jules was dancing around, dashing from one side to the other yelling for them to make up their mind, go one way or the other it didn't make any difference, just go. Their goal, the appointed staging area where they could hide the bag of seeds until the coast was clear, was only a few feet away.

In a flash everything changed for Roscoe. He realized too late the flaw in his otherwise perfect plan. He'd assumed Seed Man would put the seed bag at the base of the feeder like he usually did and not leave it in the middle of the yard. So, he had not accounted for the tree that stood in the path of the team moving the bag from where they'd picked it up to the hiding place.

Jules continued to holler, while he glanced over his shoulder to see if Seed Man was returning with his camera.

Roscoe was about to leave the command post or send Marvin down to help straighten things out when he heard something rip.

The voices on the ground grew quiet. All sound in the backyard stopped. Traffic noise from the street in front of the house dropped to a hush.

Roscoe was afraid to look. When he did he saw half the members of the seed bag team lying on their backs holding part of the sack in their paws while those on the other side held the rest of it. Between them lay a great pile of seeds dumped on the ground when the bag split open, some of it was still sliding toward their feet.

The silence was broken by the sound of Seed Man coming from the garage. He had hold of Sweetheart's hand and was pulling her along. "You've got to see this," he said excitedly. "He actually completed three turns…grabbed his paws." He was talking fast and was slightly out of breath. "Then stood…shoulders. You've just got to see this."

Sweetheart looked like she had been pulled away from cleaning the house, she still held the hose of the vacuum cleaner in her hand. She was saying, "Harold, we're having company in exactly two hours, I don't have time for this," as he pulled her closer to the tree.

The squirrels on the ground dropped the piece of the bag they were holding and scattered when they saw him. Jules, who discovered he was in the middle of the yard with no protection, walked casually around the pile of seeds and then slipped behind the tree trunk, safely out of sight.

Seed Man ran to the tree where he'd seen the acrobatic squirrels and searched the branches for them. It dawned on him they were gone about the same time he remembered why he'd come to the back yard in the first place. He looked around for the bag of seeds but didn't see it. He widened his search and finally saw pieces of the torn bag and the pile of seeds by the base of the tree.

He scratched his head and told Sweetheart he was sure he'd set the bag down where they were standing and wondered how it got over there.

"Maybe your performing squirrels did it." She shot back, pulled her hand from his and stomped back across the yard.

Seed Man stood for a moment not sure what to do. Roscoe could tell from the look on his face he was thinking he should get a scoop and a garbage bag and clean up the mess by the tree but was afraid to leave in case the two remarkable squirrels returned.

Roscoe watched him walk away then swung around and looked at the pile of seeds at the base of the tree. "Three feet," he muttered to himself. "Three feet from fame and fortune."

"Ahum," Marvin cleared his throat trying to get his attention.

"Ah, Roscoe, if it's okay with you I, ah, think I'll hop over and grab some seeds before *You-Know-Who* comes back." He made a gesture with his head toward the side of the garage. He paused for a moment to judge Roscoe's reaction, then worked his way across the yard toward the seed pile.

"To be so close to victory and lose," Roscoe mumbled as he watched Marvin walk away. His vision of a bag of seeds available whenever he wanted exploded and fell around him like an early snow. He had to make a decision about the open bag of seeds. Should he keep his resolve and insist it was all or nothing, refusing to eat what he considered to be,"Seeds of failure?" Or, should he see it as a good idea that almost worked and grab all the seeds he could carry before Seed Man returned?

He struck a pose of defiance, deciding he would be that noble squirrel who refused to settle for anything less than complete victory. He pictured a statue of himself in the very spot where he now stood commemorating the day he attempted *The Great Seed Heist*. Younger members of the Community would come and admire it. Maybe they would walk away inspired to try something big themselves. He would insist the words, *"No Compromise,"* be printed across the base of the statue.

He held his position for a moment then let his shoulders drop," Oh well," he muttered and realized he'd been so busy directing the great seed heist he'd missed breakfast. He may have failed to see all the possible obstacles in his plan but he wasn't going to let a once in a lifetime opportunity slip through his paws.

He hollered for Marvin to, "Wait up. Save some seeds for me."

"It has long been accepted by everyone in the sports community that, because of the way our bodies are constructed, we can not throw an object overhand. At best, we can only fling things in a side arm motion. Nothing in my years of coaching has changed that notion."

—From Coach Bobby's, "The Young Squirrels Complete Book of Sports."

CHAPTER 2

An Alternate Plan

When Roscoe heard about a squirrel named Rudy D who was able to throw objects overhand with uncanny accuracy, two thoughts came together in his mind. First, another piece of misinformation about squirrels had been corrected. Second, and perhaps most important was a new plan to take the bag of seeds away from Seed Man.

He knew the Flying Edelmans could not be counted on for another attempt. They'd come back a few days after the last, unsuccessful attempt to steal the seeds looking for their part of the prize. Roscoe tried to explain to them how the seed bag team had almost made it to the hiding place but the bag had ripped open when they couldn't agree on which side of a tree to go around. "No one benefited from the effort," Roscoe explained to them. But the brothers had looked at the place where they were told the incident occurred, thinking there would be some evidence of the broken bag or it's contents.

Unfortunately, Seed Man had done an amazing job of

cleaning things up, nothing was left on the ground to suggest a seed bag disaster had taken place.

"Split bag huh?" Morey asked, doubt about what they'd been told hanging on each word. "You're telling us nobody came away with anything?" Rorey shook his head in disbelief. "Who do you think we are, the Stupid Edelman Brothers?" they both asked at the same time. Morey smacked one paw into the other and told Roscoe if he ever came close to their tree again he'd knock his block off.

After they delivered their warning, he and Rorey gave Roscoe a shove to emphasize their point and took off around the corner of the house, heading back to their Neighborhood.

"I think that went rather well," Marvin said as he came from behind the tree where he'd been hiding during Roscoe's exchange with the Edelmans.

The good news was Rudy D lived in a Neighborhood close by so Roscoe didn't have to run the risk of meeting the Edelmans.

He left the first thing the next morning in search of the squirrel who could throw objects overhand.

He kept thinking this would probably end up being one of those urban legends that circulate from one neighborhood to the next which, in most cases, turns out to be false. Like the squirrel everyone said looked like Elvis. Members of his Community chased down a number of leads and discovered no one had actually seen him.

Then there was the one about Seed Man moving and taking the feeder with him. Roscoe was just a few months old when that one started but Seed Man was still coming through for them, keeping the feeder full.

Because there had been no, "eye witness," Roscoe doubted Rudy D even existed. He'd gone deep into a new Neighborhood and was moving cautiously from tree to tree, keeping an eye out for any threats to his safety. He stopped and wondered if he'd gone too far when something smacked him in the back of the head.

He spun around ready to defend himself in case whoever struck the first blow was prepared to follow it up with another. He couldn't see anything that looked suspicious so he shrugged his shoulders and figured he'd been mistaken when it happened again; something bounced off the top of his head and ricocheted off the tree next to him. This time though, he heard someone chuckling.

He finally zeroed in on the area where he heard the laughter and saw what he thought he'd never see in his life; a squirrel wearing a red warm-up jacket and matching ball cap with the bill pointing to the back.

"You Roscoe?" The squirrel in the cap asked in a surprisingly deep voice for someone his size.

"One and the same," Roscoe answered while he hopped to the ground and moved closer.

"I'm Rudy D and word has it you're looking for me." While he spoke, he tossed an acorn from one paw to the other.

"Is that what you've been throwing at me?" Roscoe pointed to the acorn.

"First time, yeah, second one was a pebble." Rudy shrugged.

While the two talked they moved closer until they were less than a foot apart.

"So?" Rudy D stopped tossing the acorn and stuck his paws into the pockets of his jacket. "What's up?"

"Well, I've got this plan that could put you in seeds for a month or so but, I need to see for myself if what they say about you is true. Can you really throw overhand?" Roscoe rubbed his chin and then folded his arms across his chest.

"I hit you didn't I?" He said it like there was nothing to hitting a moving object 15 feet away. "Twice if I'm not mistaken. What's to check out?" Rudy D looked upset that Roscoe would doubt his abilities.

"How do I know it was you doing the throwing? You might be using a sling shot, and I'll tell you right now I can't use a squirrel with a sling shot in my plan. I need someone with a strong, steady arm for the job I have in mind." Roscoe knew he was playing it close. There was a chance someone with Rudy's skills would be insulted by what he said and walk away. However something told him he was the kind of squirrel who enjoyed a challenge.

The silence after Roscoe finished seemed to last forever. Finally, Rudy D shrugged and said, "Watch this." He stepped back, went into a windup, pulled the acorn close to his chest and let it fly. A cat, sleeping on a patio in the next yard, twenty feet away, suddenly jumped up and looked around. The acorn had struck her on the top of her head.

Roscoe smiled. "What do you have going on tomorrow night?"

When he got back to his Community he brought Jules and Marvin, his two closest friends, together and went over what he decided to call his *Alternate Seed Heist Plan*.

Jules was sent out to round up as many of the original 24 members of the seed bag team he could find. After a lot of talk, he'd managed to convince most of them that Roscoe wasn't mad at them for messing up the last time and wanted them back on the team for another try.

"Tell me again why we're out here at midnight." Rudy D had his ball cap pulled low over his eyes and was tossing an acorn in the air.

"It's called a simulation, a walk through, a rehearsal if you will, of the real event scheduled for tomorrow." Roscoe had too much on his mind to keep going over the same information with team members who hadn't paid attention during the meeting earlier. Besides, Rudy D's constant acorn tossing was beginning to get on his nerves.

"I think we're good to go," Marvin had left the seed bag team and taken his place next to Roscoe.

"Does Jules have them ready? Do they know exactly what they're supposed to do this time? Did he point out alternate routes, things like that?" Roscoe held a small clipboard in his paw and was going down the list of events and the order in which they were supposed to occur.

"Well, kind of." Marvin hated to tell Roscoe anything but good news but he also knew the truth was important if they were going to have a successful practice. "A couple on the team have gone home, a few have fallen asleep and the others say they feel stupid running out and back without actually carrying anything."

"Did you tell them how important this walk through is? Did you remind them that because of their, okay, *our* mistake last time we ended up three feet short of our goal? Did you point out if we'd done this on the last operation we would have discovered the problem with the tree blocking the way to the hiding place and if we'd practiced a few times then we wouldn't be out here now?" Roscoe was leaning toward Marvin, their faces almost touching.

"Yea, I mentioned all of that but…" Marvin raised his shoulders as if to say there was only so much he could do.

"Well let's get going before we lose the rest of them." Roscoe checked his list. "Is Jules ready?"

"Affirmative," from Marvin who quickly added, "so is the target team."

Roscoe gave a low whistle and waited for a second or two. Nothing happened. He whistled a second time and got the same result.

"Marvin, would you run down and see what's holding up…" He stopped when the light on the deck of Seed Man's house came on. He could see Jules standing on one of the deck railings with his paws in the air, pumping his feet up and down. He'd completed his part of the plan, activating the motion detector but the brief celebration afterward was his idea. He jumped to the ground and ran to join what was left of the seed bag team. Roscoe heard the members of the team tell him he'd done a great job and ask if it would it be okay if they did something like that when they finished.

"Get the target team moving, we've only got thirty seconds before the light goes off." Roscoe paced back and forth; he held the clipboard in one paw and tapped it nervously against his leg.

Three squirrels carrying a long tree branch with a piece of paper stuck to the top of it, started across the yard following, as much as possible, the path Seed Man takes to the feeder. Roscoe had worked hard to get the oval piece of paper the exact height of Seed Man's head.

When the target team was half way across the yard Roscoe signaled to Rudy D who grabbed the acorn he'd been tossing, drew his arm back and fired. Hitting a sleeping cat lying on a patio was one thing but hitting a moving target six feet in the air was another. There was the problem of leading the target so the acorn and paper arrived at the same spot at the same time. There could be wind or rain to contend with, although tonight the air was calm and the sky clear.

The acorn arched through the night sky and smacked the target just above a mark Roscoe had drawn representing Seed Man's ear. The piece of paper, representing his head floated to the ground. The target team froze, they had never seen anything like it. They'd been thrown at before but had never considered the possibility that they could throw something back. The thought that one of their own could hit a moving target like that was intoxicating.

"Move it," Roscoe yelled to the target team, "the seed bag team needs to get…" Before he could finish, the twelve remaining members of the seed bag team dashed across the ground and started picking up members of the target team. The stick they were carrying fell sideways and banged against the house while the target team, overpowered by the members of the seed bag team squealed for help as they were carried to the side of the yard.

The last thing Roscoe saw before the porch light went off was Seed Man in his pajamas looking out of the big picture window trying to figure out who was making all the noise.

"Nice throw," Roscoe told Rudy D.

"No problem," he answered, checked what time he was supposed show up the next morning and took off in the dark for his Neighborhood.

At daybreak Marvin headed for the feeder and went to work. It had been a few days since Seed Man had been out so it didn't take him long to empty both feeder tubes.

He bounded back to the command post behind the low hanging branch at the back of the yard. The location gave he and Roscoe a clear view of the side of the garage without being seen. Marvin motioned for Jules to stay put, he'd taken care of the feeder himself.

Rudy D showed up on time. Because of the early morning chill he was wearing a gray sweatshirt. He had his right arm stuck in the sleeve of his red warm up jacket. "Gotta keep my shoulder warm or It'll hurt for a week," he explained when someone asked him about it.

He found Roscoe and asked, "We on for today?"

Roscoe gestured toward the base of the rose bush where the 24 members of the seed bag team waited.

"It's up to Seed Man now," Roscoe answered and told him he'd better get warmed up, things could get started at any minute.

Rudy D jogged down the little slope behind the command post and went into his stretching routine, trying to loosen up the muscles of his throwing arm.

This was the moment of every operation Roscoe loved. The hard work had been done, everything was in place and now it was just a matter of following the script he'd written.

He saw Seed Man walk up to the big picture window at the back of his house and look out. He had a cup of coffee in his hand and appeared to be checking on the condition of his trees and shrubs. His gaze stopped at the feeder and Roscoe could almost hear him thinking, "Didn't I just fill that?"

Moments later Roscoe heard the garage door go up and watched Seed Man come around the corner of the house carrying a large bag seeds under one arm.

Roscoe gave a signal with his paw and Rudy D slipped the jacket off his shoulder and went to his designated spot next to the base of an elm tree.

Seed Man whistled as he walked to the feeder. Roscoe whispered, "Now," and on cue Rudy D let loose a perfect throw. The acorn sailed toward the target and was about to make contact when the target noticed a piece of paper on the ground that had been him the night before. Because of the lack of a breeze during the night it had stayed where it landed. Roscoe realized he'd failed to assign some one the task of cleaning up the yard after their last practice. He'd assumed someone on the target team would pick it up.

Seed Man bent down to get the paper at the exact moment the acorn would have hit him in the head. He stood up unaware how close he'd come to being hit by the acorn Rudy D had thrown.

It continued on its path eventually hitting the middle of the big picture window at the back of the house. At that moment, it seemed to Roscoe, everything started moving in slow motion. There were no sounds other than a "thunk," when the acorn hit the window. He watched Seed Man turn his head slowly to see what had made the noise.

Roscoe and Marvin watched helplessly from the command post.

The big picture window vibrated for a second, grew still and then exploded into a thousand pieces. Large chunks of glass flew through the air and then broke into smaller ones as they hit the ground. Sunlight glistened off the shards lying in the grass.

Then things returned to normal speed as the seed bag team, hearing the acorn hit the window and thinking it had hit Seed Man, sprang into action. The ran toward the middle of the yard with their heads down, concentrating on the task at hand, determined not to make the same mistake they'd made the last time.

They grabbed the first thing they came to. Seed Man yelled as the twenty four squirrels surrounded him, took hold of his pant legs and started pulling.

He called for Sweetheart, his wife, or anyone who could help him fight off the attacking squirrels.

He started to loose his balance and to keep from falling dropped the bag of seeds. It hit the ground with a thud and broke open.

The seed bag team stopped, confused by the sound of the bag hitting the ground and the seeds bouncing around them. Somewhere between the acorn hitting the window and the bag hitting the ground they put two and two together and wondered if the bag was on the ground next to them what did they have hold of ? When they realized it was the legs of Seed Man's pants they squealed, let go and took off, looking for the quickest way to the tall grass at the back of the yard.

Seed Man regained his balance and was caught between concern for his window and worry the squirrels would return and attack again. He decided his best course of action was to get inside the house as quickly as possible and call his insurance man about the window, he'd take care of the seeds later.

Roscoe had watched the whole thing play out in front of him like a bad dream. But, he thought if the seed bag team could be reassembled quickly enough there was still a chance to salvage some of the seeds. He sent Marvin and Jules to round them up but, after searching for a few minutes, they were only able to find six of the original twenty four members. Two of them struggled, trying to break loose from Marvin's grasp.

"Let them go," Roscoe told him, there was a tone of defeat in his voice. His dream of having his own bag of seeds in his nest, available whenever he wanted a snack, had ended in failure for a second time.

"Ah, I think I'll take off," Rudy D had his sweatshirt folded over his arm and was standing below the command post. "Sorry about the, ah, you know." He couldn't bring himself to admit he'd missed his target and hit the window.

"Right, thanks Rudy, you had no way of knowing he'd reach for the piece of paper." Roscoe sighed, "It's not your fault."

Rudy D said he'd see him around and left.

"Roscoe, if you don't mind, I think I'll…" Marvin nodded his head toward the broken seed bag on the ground.

"Sure," Roscoe answered, "be my guest."

He'd kicked himself after the last effort for giving up and eating what he had called the, "Seeds of Defeat." He'd seen it as a sign of personal weakness and vowed it would never happen again. He'd rather starve than join the others on the ground, filling up on the seeds that spilled from the bag.

He sat in his command post the picture of defeat; his head was down and his arms were folded across his chest. He was staring straight ahead but seeing nothing.

He heard others from the Community join the group on the ground as word of his second failure began to spread. A couple of the members from the seed bag team tried to pull part of the sack to safety, hoping to salvage something good from their efforts. It was too heavy for them and they couldn't get the others to stop eating long enough to help.

Marvin jumped in beside him. "High grade seeds Roscoe. I'd say the quality is," he tapped his chin like he was trying to make a big decision, "A+." When he finally spoke his voice had a dreamy quality to it. He'd been up since dawn and this was his second feeding, the first was when he drained the feeder tubes and set the operation in motion.

He needed a nap.

"A+ quality?" Roscoe replayed Marvin's comments. "High grade seeds?" He said and twitched his tail.

He left the command post and headed for the broken bag in the center of the yard. *"Valiantly the brave young squirrel snatched the A+, high grade seeds of victory from the jaws of defeat."*

He told himself to remember that line and to make sure it was included if anyone ever wrote a story about this period in his life.

CHAPTER 3
A Plan Revised

The members of the Committee for the Protection of Neighborhood Resources take their jobs seriously. To even be considered for a place on the Committee requires performing some notable act of service for the Community. The number of Committee members is spelled out in the *Big Book of Important Things* kept locked away in the library. Membership on the Committee is for life, so openings are few and far between.

It was no little thing then when Roscoe was called before the Committee to explain his actions in the two failed attempts to secure the bag of seeds from Seed Man. "Attempts," Edgar, chairperson of the Committee explained dramatically in his opening remarks, "in which you put members of our Community, yes, perhaps the very existence of our beloved Community in danger, because of your selfish desire for personal gain."

That was the hardest part for Roscoe to take. He could understand how they might see his actions as selfish, even though others would have benefited. His dream of reaching for a bag of seeds in the corner of his nest first thing in the morning instead of traipsing across frozen, snow covered ground to feeder tubes that may or may not contain seeds had been the motivation in the two previous attempts. Efforts, from his point of view, that would have succeeded if it hadn't been for the failure of others to work together and follow his instructions.

He knew they would find him guilty; it's hard to make a convincing argument for innocence when your faced with 24 eyewitnesses from the seed bag team. He figured there was a pretty good chance he would get off with a dropping, a practice where members of the Committee drop acorns on someone believed to have endangered the Community. He was pretty sure he could survive that.

The worst possible ruling would be banishment, a verdict that would send him to another Neighborhood and force him to live in a different Community. The Committee had only used banishment once when Manfred, a member of the Community of Abner had fallen in love with Doreen from the Community of Ben, an act strictly forbidden in the Community by-laws.

If they had thought to ask Abner about it he probably would have said he wished they'd never put that part in the Community rules. But, he was on vacation when the decision to banish was made so all the Committee had to go on was what was written in *The Big Book of Important Things*.

Even though he had been very young, Roscoe remembered the day the banishment took place. Members of the Community lined up in two rows and stood silently as Manfred walked between them with his head down. He continued across the line that separates the two Communities where a weeping Doreen waited.

Manfred's parents were torn between supporting him and their love for the Community. "When Manfred left," his mother told a reporter from *The Abner Echo*, the local newspaper, "part of me was banished too. The penalty is too severe and must be changed."

"The decision of the Committee," Edgar announced, pulling Roscoe back from his thoughts, "is to issue a warning of the harshest measure to you Roscoe. We've decided to take it easy this time because of your youth and inexperience but, if you make any further attempt to capture the seed bag the consequences will be dire. Indeed, most dire." He gave Roscoe a hard look.

"However, to make sure you have learned a lesson from all this you will be subjected to a Committee screeching and then released. Any further attempt on your part to obtain seeds by other than traditional means, and by that I mean removing them from the feeder tubes one at a time, will result in a far more serious punishment." Edgar paused and gave Roscoe time to think about what he'd done and the punishment he was about to receive. "Do you understand the ruling of the Committee?"

"Sure, I mean, yes sir," Roscoe answered meekly. In a screeching, each Committee member walks by the accused and gives his fiercest screech, a sound squirrel's normally make when they're angry or frightened. The idea behind the punishment is that the transgressor will remember the sound of the screeching the next time he thinks about repeating any act that endangers the Community.

As Roscoe thought about it, he decided the punishment could have been a lot worse.

He stood at attention, head bowed slightly, as one by one the respected members of the Committee stopped in front of him and screeched. The fourth member was performing his duty when Roscoe felt a piece of paper slip into his paw.

When it was over and he was dismissed he went back to his nest, relieved he was not at the moment rubbing bruises on the top of his head caused by falling acorns when he remembered the piece of paper he'd been handed. He wasn't sure which of the Committee members gave it to him other than he knew it wasn't Edgar.

He unfolded the paper and read, "Mt, bg elm, mnite." The note had been written hurriedly and there was no name or clue of any kind whether it was midnight tonight or tomorrow night. It didn't say which of the many elm trees in the Neighborhood the writer was talking about. And, Roscoe wondered why someone on the Committee would want to meet with him anyway? Was this a test to see if he'd learned his lesson?

He stood at the base of an elm tree at what he guessed was midnight. The moon was in the right position and Seed Man had turned the lights off in his house and gone to bed.

"Psst." He heard something but it was hard to tell if it was a normal night sound or one that had been made on purpose. He heard it again and started to turn, it seemed to be coming form behind him, on the other side of the tree.

"That's far enough, keep looking at Seed Man's house." The voice was so quiet, Roscoe had to strain to hear what was said.

"What's the problem?" Roscoe whispered. "The others are asleep. Nobody's going to…" It bothered him he couldn't see who he was talking to.

"They could be watching, I'm not sure. I didn't stay for the meeting after the screeching." The whispering voice paused but before Roscoe could ask, "Who could be watching?" it continued. "Several of us admire what you've done Roscoe.

Some on the Committee pushed for a dropping but we talked them out of it."

Roscoe didn't know if he should say thanks or not, the screeching had been pretty embarrassing. He felt almost as stupid now, standing at the base of a tree, talking to the empty space in front of him.

"Someone needs to strike a blow for independence. We cannot be subject to the whims of Seed Man forever." Roscoe thought he detected a tone of anger in the speakers voice. "I will say two things to you and leave. I believe you're creative enough to figure out what to do."

Roscoe turned slightly so he could hear the speaker better.

"First, take the feeder tube, not the seed bag." The voice stopped, waiting to make sure Roscoe understood.

"But the feeder is six feet in the air and you have to lift it over the hook which means it has to go even higher. And don't forget, it's held on with a plastic tie." Taking the feeder tube made no sense to him. It had to weigh a couple of pounds when it's full. That would take half a dozen squirrels just to lift it and then what would they do once they had it? If they dropped it seeds would end up all over the ground and nothing would be accomplished.

His thoughts were interrupted as the voice behind him continued. "The second thing is, Manny."

"Manny?" Roscoe said out loud. "Fat Manny? Manny the seed eating machine? Manny, I'm so big I can't get out of my nest so you're going to have to bring the seeds to me Manny? You can't be serious."

"Look, this conversation is over. I've given you all you need to…" The voice stopped when the light on the back of Seed Man's house came on apparently triggered by the motion detector. Someone must have been watching and tried to move closer to hear what was being said. When they did, they activated the light.

Roscoe heard the sound of the midnight messenger climbing the tree behind him and realized he'd never know who the voice belonged to or who his admirers on the Committee were.

He saw a crumpled scrap of paper close to his feet and reached to pick it up when he heard the sound of someone walking across Seed Man's yard towards him.

"A little late for a young squirrel to be out if you ask me." Roscoe caught the face of Edgar just before the porch light clicked off.

"Ah, well, see, I, ah, couldn't sleep and thought I'd, you know, take a walk and try to settle down." Roscoe was having trouble adjusting to the change from how bright it was when the porch light was on to how dark it was with it off. That, and having Edgar suddenly appear out of nowhere caused his thinking to get a little fuzzy.

"And talking to someone, I believe." Edgar moved uncomfortably close as far as Roscoe was concerned. "If I'm not mistaken I heard voices, more than one I think."

"Voices? Ah, no, I don't think so. I was just saying, ah, how thoughtless I had been to endanger the Community, is all. I didn't hear anyone else, really." Roscoe hoped Edgar hadn't seen him pick up the piece of paper. He couldn't remember if he'd done it before the light went off or not.

"Very well Roscoe, I'll assume it is as you say. But, I'd suggest you scamper off to bed now, it will be morning soon." Edgar's voice took on a more fatherly tone, showing concern for what happens to sleepy squirrels in daylight. "We wouldn't want to get caught by any wild things tomorrow because we couldn't stay awake, would we?"

"No indeed sir. Thank you." Roscoe turned to go. Had he just been given a warning from a respected leader in the Community or was it a threat?

"Ah, Roscoe," Edgar's voice changed and became more serious.

"Yes sir."

"We're keeping an eye on you, the other members of the Committee and I." Edgar pointed to his eyes with his paw and then at Roscoe, to emphasize they'd be watching him. "I'd watch my step if I were you." A long pause followed the warning then Edgar turned and walked away.

"Right," Roscoe answered over his shoulder as he cut across the back of Seed Man's yard to his nest.

He couldn't sleep. He tried different positions, fluffed the grass under his head, but nothing helped. He was disturbed by what the mysterious voice had told him and it was too dark to see anything on the paper thrown his way when the porch light came on.

He waited until the first rays of sunlight broke through the tree limbs over head, then paced back and forth in his nest as members of the Community got up and went to the feeder for breakfast.

When it was quiet again and he was sure no one would pop over the side of his nest to see what he was doing, he opened the paper. He saw a crudely drawn sketch and it didn't take a genius to figure out it was meant to show the squirrel feeder. He could make out the rod stuck in the ground. He followed it to the top where it split into two arcs, going in opposite directions. He traced one of the arcs with a paw as it looped down and back up again where it formed a natural hook for the wire support on the feeder tube.

He scratched his head. "What? There's nothing new here. I've been to the feeder since I was a baby, I know it like I know every tree limb in the neighborhood."

He tossed the paper aside and tried to figure out why the voice would want to meet him in the middle of the night, tell him he was admired by several members of the Committee, run the risk of being caught out of his nest after dark, given two useless suggestions and a sketch that didn't make any sense.

He glanced back at the paper on the floor of his nest and noticed, it had fallen with the other side facing him. He saw something he'd missed when he was looking at it the first time. He picked it up and looked closer. It was another sketch of the feeder only this time the rod was bent to the point that the bottom of one of the feeding tubes almost touched the ground.

On top of one of the looping rods that held the tube was a huge shape which, even badly drawn, was meant to be a very large squirrel.

"Manny?" he whispered. Then it hit him and he said a little louder, "Manny, of course."

The good news was to get to Manny's nest Roscoe didn't have to leave the Neighborhood. The bad news was Manny was not the friendliest squirrel in the Community. Maybe it was his weight problem, or maybe it was his attitude that caused him to have a weight problem, Roscoe didn't know. What he did know was no one wanted to have anything to do with him.

Roscoe worked his way up the tree trunk and around the branches Manny had arranged at odd angles to discourage visitors.

He hoped he could get close enough to talk to him.

His head was almost even with the bottom of his nest when he heard Manny's rough, gravelly voice say, "Who ever you are stop and turn around or your going to get hurt." Manny was a squirrel with a limited vocabulary and the few words he did know weren't nice.

"Oh, hey Manny, it's me, Roscoe." He tried to sound casual like he'd suddenly become aware he'd climbed the wrong tree.

"So?" Manny didn't offer any encouragement.

"So, ah, I was just passing by and thought I'd come up and…"

"Knock it off Rosc," Manny interrupted him, "no one just happens to drop by my place." Roscoe heard a huge tail smack against the side of the nest. He figured Manny was rolling to one side to get a better look at him.

"You got me. You're right. I didn't come up the wrong tree but I did want to talk to you about something." He hoped he'd said enough to make him curious.

"Like?"

"Well, let me put it this way, it involves seeds." Roscoe climbed a little higher. He could actually see over the top of the nest and into Manny's small beady eyes. "Lots of seeds."

"So?"

"Well, so, I had this idea that would take maybe, ten minutes of your time and lets say, provide a juicy reward for your effort." Since Manny hadn't stopped him he inched a little higher. He could see into the nest, at least he thought there was a nest there, mostly what he saw was Manny. He was huge, bigger than Roscoe had remembered from the last time he'd seen him.

"How juicy?" Even though his question was followed by a yawn, Roscoe could tell he was interested.

"Say, a handful of seeds juicy." Roscoe tried to make a handful sound like it was a big deal.

"No can do Rosc," Manny answered, "I'd take the easy way down if I was you, it'd be a shame to fall to the ground, if you get my drift." Roscoe saw his gigantic shape, roll to one side. He knew he had to have this guy on his team, he was the only one in the Community big enough to bend the rod and bring the feeder tube close to the ground.

"Did you have a figure in mind? I mean, I'm flexible here." Roscoe thought that was the best he could do, throw a little hook out there and see what he might catch.

"Well, let's think about it okay?" Manny tilted his head so he was looking directly at Roscoe. "I gotta climb down the tree, right? You want me to do something while I'm on the ground, then I gotta climb back up the tree. No way I'm doing that for a handful of seeds."

"So, what are we talking about here?" Roscoe thought it best for Manny to make an offer.

"One third of whatever you're going after or I don't budge. You got a problem with that consider our discussion over." After delivering his final offer, Manny rolled over so all Roscoe could see was his giant back.

"Me? A problem? No sir, no problem here, I can live with that," Roscoe replied, "so here's what I have in mind." He pulled out the sketch he'd picked up the night before and held it up for Manny to see. He went over the details of the operation, talked about the time it would start and then, after getting a nod of approval from him said, "See you around."

"Ah, Rosc," Manny's voice caught him as he was about to turn and head down the tree.

"Yeah?"

"Don't make a habit of dropping by my place, you see what I'm saying?" The mean tone had slipped back into his voice.

"No problem whatsoever, message received and filed away in the old memory bank." Roscoe touched a paw to his head and climbed down the tree, he had no intention of coming back any time soon.

Roscoe knew the timetable he'd given Manny was tight and he had a lot of things to do before the operation started. There was also the problem of Edgar's comment about being watched by members of the Committee, so he had to be careful not to appear to be planning anything. Trying to explain to twenty-four squirrels what they were supposed to do would have been impossible to conceal but for this operation he only needed four.

He quietly went around and spoke to the ones he'd chosen then met with them in the open, appearing to be a group of friends playing around on a warm, sunlit afternoon. As they jumped, rolled and chased each other up and down tree trunks, he explained their role in stealing the feeder tube.

"The main thing is it can't look like I have anything to do with this," Roscoe explained. "In fact, while you're getting the feeder tube, I plan to be paying our Committee Chairman a visit and asking if there's some Community service I can do to make up for the terrible misdeeds of my past. So, from here on in, you're on your own."

They nodded they understood and told him not to worry about a thing. Before they took off they formed a circle, touched paws and said, "Seeds."

Roscoe is a natural worrier. He'd been tripped up on his last two efforts by little mistakes. He'd failed to see a tree in the path that prevented the seed bag team from getting the sack to the hiding place on the first attempt and failed to assign someone the task of picking up a piece of paper in the second that caused Seed Man to bend down and miss getting hit by the acorn thrown by Rudy D.

"Where's the flaw in this one?" He spent most of the morning in his nest going over each part of the plan in his mind and couldn't find one. He'd checked the sketch he'd been given half a dozen times to make sure he understood it. The beauty of the plan was in its simplicity, it only involved five squirrels instead of the twenty-four required in the last plan.

It can't fail, he told himself. Manny climbs the rod to the feeders, gets into position, the rod bends lowering the tube, the feeder team runs out, lifts the tube off the hook and dashes to a prearranged hiding place. Manny climbs down the pole and goes back to his nest while the feeder team disappears into the woods.

He couldn't find a weak point in the entire plan.

It was almost time for things to get under way so Roscoe climbed down his tree and headed over to Edgar's. Out of the corner of his eye he could see Manny ambling slowly to the feeder. Nothing unusual here, other than the fact the Manny never ambles to the feeder but forces others to amble there and get seeds for him.

If anyone in the Community thought of standing up to him and saying, "Get your own seeds," he would whisper to them in his raspy voice, "You can run all you want but you'll have to sleep sometime and when you do…" He would tilt his head to one side, close his eyes and let the offending member guess what it would be like to wake up in the middle of the night to find Manny in their nest.

While he waited at the base of Edgar's tree he saw Manny start up the feeder rod. Half way up he had to stop to catch his breath and for a brief moment Roscoe saw his perfect plan end right there. He was glad he'd told the feeder team to wait until the bottom of the feeder tube touches the ground before leaving their cover beneath the rose bush.

The Squirrel Chronicles: Book One

Then to Roscoe's relief Manny started climbing again, spurred on by the thought of feasting on the third of a tube of seeds he'd be getting for a few minutes work. For Roscoe though it was no longer about the seeds but recovering his severely damaged credibility.

Edgar called down, asking Roscoe what he wanted.

While he was telling Edgar about his plan to volunteer for Community service and in some small way make up for his past misdeeds, he saw Manny reach the top of the feeder rod and start toward the arm holding the tube.

He watched the rod start to bend as Manny moved farther out. The bottom of the feeder tube got close to the ground and he could see the feeder team get into their starting position.

Edgar was saying something about thinking it best if he brought his request to the whole Committee when Roscoe allowed himself the luxury of thinking about the success of the plan and the fulfillment of the dream of having a pile of seeds tucked in the corner of his nest.

Edgar asked if Roscoe understood what he'd said since there had been a long pause after he'd told him about appearing before the Committee.

Roscoe saw the feeder team start across the yard. He knew they were fast but he also knew it would take several seconds for them to make it to the feeder.

"Don't look up Manny," Roscoe whispered, "please, don't look up."

Edgar hollered for Roscoe to speak louder, he hadn't heard what he said. At the same time Edgar asked Roscoe to talk louder Manny, not sure what to do until the feeder team arrived, looked up.

He saw, no more than six feet away, the largest squirrel he

had ever seen staring back at him. Wiser, smarter squirrels would have recognized at once it was their own reflection in the big picture window at the back of Seed Man's house. Every squirrel who came to the feeder for the first time had to work through the moment of panic that came over them the first time they saw their reflection in the glass.

It had been a long time since Manny had come to the feeder, he'd been younger then and much smaller. Since then he forced others to get seeds for him so hadn't worried about things like thinking his reflection was another squirrel. In a way, he was having the experience for the first time.

He'd always gotten his way by being the biggest and meanest squirrel in the Community. Smaller squirrels did what he said or ran the risk of getting clobbered. He'd been known to push a young seed school student to the ground and sit on him until he said he'd go to the feeder and get seeds for him.

Suddenly Manny was looking at a squirrel who appeared to be as big and mean as he was.

While he was experiencing his first touch of fear the Feeder Team had crossed the yard and grabbed hold of the bottom of the feeder tube. They spaced themselves well, dividing the bottom of the tube into four sections and getting a good grip on the part in front of them. They bent their knees and raised their arms, preparing to lift.

Manny leaned forward and watched the squirrel opposite him do the same. He nodded his head in a fierce way, a gesture squirrels use when they're ready to fight.

The feeder team felt their feet leave the ground as Manny shifted his weight on top of the pole.

The squirrel opposite him did the same thing and seemed unfazed by his gestures. Manny stood on his back legs and brought his arms up ready to fight. So did his opponent.

The feet of the feeder team returned to the ground and they prepared to lift the tube off the hook thinking this was the time to remove the feeder.

Somewhere between nodding his head and forming his paws into fists Manny lost his balance and fought to right himself but failed. Fortunately for him, he wasn't far from the ground. Even with such a short fall he hit with a thud and lay on his back for a moment expecting the other squirrel to pounce on him and finish off what he'd started.

He looked up with a sense of relief when he realized the other squirrel had gone, apparently frightened when he took a swing at him.

When no attack came, he rolled over awkwardly and started across the yard as fast as his big body and little legs could carry him. He gave no thought to what would happened to the those who were lifting the feeder tube when he fell; he was totally focused on the single thought of getting back to his nest as fast as possible.

With the removal of Manny's weight the rod that had been nearly bent in two moments before, sprang back to its original position flinging the members of the feeder team still holding on to the feeder tube across the yard at speeds none of them had experienced before. They landed in the soft ground in the middle of Seed Man's garden.

While they were spread out on the ground trying to recover from what they'd just experienced the feeder tube they'd clung to for most of their flight slammed into the ground and somersaulted across the garden eventually coming to rest underneath an evergreen.

It didn't take them long to put two and two together and

began grabbing the seeds that had spilled on the ground around them.

Others from the Community who'd been watching the event scrambled across the yard to join in the feast.

"What was that?" Edgar called from his nest. "I heard something. It sounded like a heavy object hitting the ground."

"Heard something sir? An object you say? Hitting…" Roscoe was backing away from Edgar's tree as he talked. He knew something had gone wrong, there was nothing in his plan that called for a heavy object to hit anything.

Edgar stood in his nest and scanned the area around him. He stopped when he came to the squirrel feeder and saw one of the feeding tubes was missing. The rod holding the remaining tube were still swaying violently back and forth.

"Roscoe, so help me if I discover you had anything to do with this,…" Edgar was climbing down the tree hollering at him.

Roscoe gave him a look that asked how could he possibly be involved, he'd been talking with him the whole time?

Edgar ran to the feeder to investigate while Roscoe made his way back to his tree and curled up in his nest.

One mistake he could live with. The second one really bothered him. He knew in this Community it was three strikes and your out; no one he knew would be willing to follow a three time loser.

He picked the piece of paper with the diagram off the floor of his nest. It showed the pole bent and the feeder tube inches from the ground. Even though he'd studied the sketch carefully he saw, for the first time, the midnight messenger had scrawled a note at the bottom of it. He pulled the page closer and scooted to a spot where the light was better.

"PS: B sure M's looking away from PW."

He knew the M stood Manny and figured the PW meant picture window.

He tossed the note into a corner of his nest and turned his back to it.

His stomach growled and he realized he'd been so busy organizing the operation and instructing others on what they were supposed to do, he'd missed both breakfast and lunch.

He remembered the last thing he'd seen as he was leaving Edgar's tree were dozens of Community members running across the Clearing toward Seed Man's garden.

He doubted there were any seeds left.

He crawled out of his nest and started down the tree.

"It won't hurt to check it out," he muttered and joined the others in a dash across the Clearing and up the path to Seed Man's yard.

CHAPTER 4
A Change of Plans

    Roscoe hadn't left his nest in two days; he just didn't feel like going out. He kept replaying the three failed attempts to improve his seed situation in his mind and after each review he felt worse. He'd come so close. He'd failed to pick up a piece of paper in one and to read a tiny note at the bottom of a page in another. Little things had kept him from achieving his goal of a bag of seeds in his nest within easy reach on cold, wintry mornings. He was three feet from victory in one case and a reflection in a window in another.

    He didn't think he could take any more ribbing from the Community so he hadn't gone out. Fortunately, unlike elephants, squirrels have short memories. But then elephants aren't seed eaters and, now that he thought about it, Edgar, Chairman of the Committee To Protect Neighborhood Resources, knew every detail of his life like a book.

    He sighed and put his head on his paws.

    "Ah, Roscoe, sorry for interrupting your, ah, whatever it is

The Squirrel Chronicles: Book One

you're doing there, but you have a guest, guests actually." Roscoe had been so engrossed in his own thoughts he hadn't heard his friend Marvin come up the tree and take a position on a limb next to him.

"Tell whoever it is to go away, I don't exactly feel like talking to anyone at the moment." He barely had enough energy to lift his head off his paws how could he possibly carry on a conversation.

"Well, see, I don't think, ah, you can do that." Marvin was caught between bothering his friend and making him realize you just can't say you don't want to see Edgar and the Committee when they stop by for a visit.

"Mmmm…" is all Roscoe could say.

"See, it's, ah, don't get upset at me for saying this Roscoe but it's, Edgar." Marvin moved a little farther away, afraid Roscoe might throw something at him.

"Edgar? Why would he want to talk to me? Unless he thought I…"

"They've talked to Manny," Marvin volunteered then added quickly, "but they haven't talked to Jules or me yet."

Roscoe sat up, moved slowly to the edge of his nest and looked down. He saw Edgar on the ground pacing back and forth. Four members of the Committee stood to one side, careful not to get in his way.

Roscoe got out of his nest and worked his way down the tree. You don't say no to the Committee Chairman no matter how bad you feel. As soon as his feet touched the ground he said, "I think I know why you're here and okay, I…"

That was as far as he got when Darin, a Committee member, sneezed. When he was sure Roscoe was looking at him, he drew a paw across his throat.

Roscoe didn't get it.

"Look, I know there have been problems in the past but I…" Roscoe tried again but had to stop when Darin started coughing, like a seed was caught in his throat. When Roscoe looked at him he shook his head no, and put a paw to his lips.

"You wanted to see me Edgar?" Roscoe asked, wondering if Darin was the one who'd slipped him the sketch that night in the dark.

"Yes, Roscoe my boy, that we have." He turned to those with him and said, "What a smart lad, he figured it out immediately." His tone was friendly and as he spoke he closed the distance between them and put an arm around Roscoe's shoulders. "First, I hope you notice I said, *we've* come to see *you*. Hmmm?" He looked at Roscoe and raised his eyebrows hoping he would catch the significance of what he was saying. "Notice we did not *send* for you."

Roscoe swallowed. Something weird was going on. "I, ah, understand you've talked to Manny." He hadn't meant to say it but he felt uncomfortable with Edgar standing inches away with his arm resting on his shoulder. He was so close, Roscoe saw the fur on his chest move when he breathed.

"True. Quite a character that Manny but finally, after hours of questioning he admitted it was his idea to sit on top of the feeder. He said it was an accident, he hadn't been there in some time and made a beginners mistake, looking at the window and seeing his reflection. He had no idea why the four Community members who ended up in Seed Man's garden tried to grab the feeder when it was close to the ground. Nor did he think he could pick them out of a lineup if we got a group of the usual suspects together." Roscoe thought he heard something in Edgar's voice that said he wasn't sure he believed him.

"But, that's as they say, hulls under a different feeder. There is something we want to talk to you about though." Edgar turned Roscoe so he was facing the back of Seed Man's house. "Tell me what you see Roscoe."

"Well I see grass, flowers, Seed Mans house of course, and then there's…"

"Let me rephrase my question Roscoe and see if it helps." Edgar waited for a moment to let his frustration cool down then asked, "What don't you see?"

"What don't I… Oh, you mean like the feeder?" Roscoe took a closer look. The feeder support pole and both feeder tubes were gone. He scanned the backyard thinking Seed Man must have moved them to a different place.

"It's gone. The feeders gone." It had always been there, as long as he could remember. It was the kind of thing you wouldn't notice missing unless someone pointed it out to you.

"There's a Committee meeting tonight Roscoe dealing with this very issue. I, that is, we, the Committee and I, strongly urge you attend." He gave Roscoe's shoulder a squeeze and left with the rest of the Committee.

"Where do we meet? What time is the meeting? Who else is going to…" Roscoe stopped as he watched Edgar and the Committee walk away. Save your breath, he told himself, he's not listening.

At dusk, when most squirrels are shaping their nest and getting ready for a good nights sleep, Roscoe stood in front of the door to the Committee meeting room. He started to knock but the door opened while his paw was still in the air and was hurried inside by the sergeant-of-arms. After pulling him into the room, the sergeant-of-arms looked outside, making sure Roscoe hadn't been followed, then closed the door.

The room was smaller than Roscoe remembered, a fact made worse by the number of those who sat or stood around the edges of it. He looked around in disbelief. He saw the Flying Edelmans, Morey and Rorey. On the other side of the room he could see Rudy D, still wearing his ball cap. And, taking up almost all of one corner was Mannny.

"I get it. I see what's going on." Roscoe started backing towards the door. "It's a banishment isn't it? You brought me in here…" he spun around and tried to make a break for the door but the sergeant-at-arms grabbed him and said, "Take it easy Roscoe. Hear what he has to say."

While Roscoe struggled to free himself from the grip of the sergeant-at-arms Edgar stood. "There will be no talk of banishment tonight Roscoe. We have a much bigger problem before us than reviewing your youthful indiscretions." Edgar dropped his head and clasped his paws behind his back demonstrating the gravity of the situation facing them.

"Sorry we threatened you Roscoe," Rorey was the first to speak. "Edgar pointed out how the seed bag broke and that Seed Man cleaned it up."

"We didn't believe it could happen like that, but we do now." Morey finished his sentence.

"Sorry," they both said, bent their knees and pushed off, completing a flip in the air and landing where they'd started.

"Me to," Rudy D added, "I should have thought about the window and waited until he was clear. It was a rookie mistake."

"Ditto," Manny said.

"So," Edgar looked around at the room and then back at Roscoe, "what are *you* going to do about the missing feeder situation?"

Everyone in the room, except Manny started giving Roscoe their opinion about what should be done.

"Stop," Manny's deep, husky voice stunned them to silence. "Let Roscoe speak." Manny doesn't say much but when he does it carries a lot of weight.

"Let me speak about what?" Roscoe was confused, "Do what? I have no idea what you're talking about."

"You've tried some, how shall I say it, unusual things in the past to solve a, ah, personal seed problem if I'm not mistaken." While Edgar talked he straightened a picture of himself, drawn the day he became Chairman. He dusted the top of the frame with his elbow then turned to Roscoe. "I, that is, the Committee and I want you to apply those same creative skills of yours in solving a grave Community problem. Does that shed some light on the situation?"

Before Roscoe could say anything Edgar moved to a place in front of him. "Someone once said, 'Where there are no seeds the squirrels perish." He put a paw on Roscoe's shoulder and walked him over to the only window in the room. "The continued existence of our beloved Community is in your paws son." Edgar turned away, not wanting Roscoe or the others to see him so emotional.

Roscoe swallowed and thought, "It's about the missing feeder isn't it?"

Edgar nodded yes and asked, "When can we expect a plan? You have the undying loyalty and cooperation of everyone in this room. Am I right?"

"Right," everyone answered. The Edelman brothers hopped up and down to emphasize their commitment.

"First thing in the morning, sir." Roscoe was overwhelmed by the confidence they'd shown in him. "Ah, is Sparky available?"

"As I've mentioned, all the resources of the Community are at your disposal." Edgar made a motion for the sergeant-at-arms to get Sparky and have him at Roscoe's nest after the meeting.

"Now, let's go over what we know." Edgar had regained his composure, walked to the meeting room table and picked up a paper that held the notes he'd made. "Seed Man is not in the Neighborhood." A gasp came from those in the small room, this was a new piece of information for them. For years they'd lived in the fear of Seed Man leaving and taking the feeder with him "But," Edgar continued over the buzz of conversation, "we know he'll be back because the people next door are taking care of his cat. And, whatever we do must be done quickly because we have no idea when he'll return."

The rest of the meeting was taken up with details like whether the Edelman's should stay with someone in the Community overnight or go to their Neighborhood and come back in the morning. Eventually they decided to go home and wait until they got word that Roscoe had come up with a workable plan.

Edgar adjourned the meeting but told everyone to be available for another meeting, "At a moment's notice." He crossed the room and stood next to Roscoe. "Plan well my boy, you are the last, best hope of our beloved Community." He stood quietly for a moment with his face inches from Roscoe's. He could see a tear that form in his eye, break loose and roll down his cheek. Then he straightened and walked out of the room unable to say another word.

As those at the meeting filed out they passed by Roscoe, patted him on the back and said they were sure he'd come up with something.

When everyone had gone Roscoe stood alone in the room wishing he had as much confidence in himself as the others did.

When he got back to his tree Sparky was standing near the

trunk. Sparky is that odd member every Community has who doesn't quite fit in because he doesn't think like everyone else. He's a technical thinker so for him, everything breaks down to a few simple rules he knows backwards and forwards. He keeps his fur longer than the others, matted in spots and mostly gone from the top of his head because of his a habit of tugging on it when he's solving a problem. While others see a falling acorn and rush to bury it before winter arrives, Sparky wonders what made it go down instead of up and how fast it was falling when it hit the ground. He would try to predict how high it will go after it lands and how many times it will bounce before it comes to rest.

In other words, Sparky is the Community nerd.

"You wanted to see me Roscoe?" His voice is surprisingly high pitched and cracked occasionally because he spends more time thinking than talking.

"Simply put Sparky, we need to find a way to get into Seed Man's garage." Roscoe knew it would only confuse things if he didn't state the problem simply and concisely. He also knew if he said too much, Sparky would continue to press for details of the plan which at the moment, he would be unable answer.

"No problem. Catch you in the morning."

Before Roscoe could say thanks or ask if he needed any help, he was gone.

The next morning Roscoe woke up and came down his tree to go for an early breakfast, the way his day was shaping up he didn't know when he'd have another chance to get something to eat. He was surprised to find Sparky standing in the same place they'd met the night before. There were dark circles under his eyes and his face was blotchy; it was obvious he'd had very little sleep.

He yawned before he spoke.

"Here you go Roscoe." It was so typical of Sparky Roscoe thought. There was no mention that he'd stayed up all night. Nothing was said about how hard he'd worked or how difficult solving the problem had been.

"What are they?" Roscoe held two small, gray boxes in his paw. One of them had a button on top, the other had straps coming out each side.

"Oh, yea, I see." Sparky had trouble remembering others weren't able to figure things out as quickly as he did. "Well, the first one opens the garage door and the other one, the one with the straps, allows us to talk to each other."

"How do they work?" Roscoe was amazed that things like this could be built at all let alone overnight.

"Well if you know the frequency of the garage door then with a rheostat you can dial down the…"

"No, no, no," Roscoe waved his free hand trying to slow Sparky down. He was sure any explanation he gave would be way over his head. "What I mean is what do I have to do to make them work?"

"Oh, right. See that one?" he pointed to the box with a red button on top. "You push that and the garage door will open. If I had more time I could make it go down but…" He shrugged suggesting under the time restraints he could only do so much.

"And the other?" Roscoe held up the one with the two straps.

"Push here when you want to talk," he pointed to an orange button on the side, "and let up to listen. That's about it."

Roscoe sent word to Edgar to schedule a meeting. With the two devices Sparky had come up with and a piece of paper that outlined his plan to put the feeders back into action, he headed to the meeting.

"What it boils down to is we go in the garage, find the feeder pole and tubes and put them back up just like nothing ever happened." Roscoe had shown his sketches to the Committee members and outlined his plan to them. They had a number of questions about how many would be involved, who would direct the effort and if he thought they'd be finished in time for an afternoon snack.

"I'm thinking we do it tonight," Roscoe answered. "It will probably take that long to get every thing in place."

Sparky put a paw in the air. "You may have forgotten one thing Roscoe."

If it hadn't been Sparky asking the question Roscoe would have been prepared for criticism. Everyone in the Community was aware that in each of his failed attempts he had made one small mistake. However, he knew Sparky didn't think like the others, he was only interested in the technical side of things getting into personal issues was not his style.

"What are you talking about Sparky?" Most in the Community wrote Sparky off as "weird" and would have dismissed what he had to say. So they were surprised when Roscoe pressed him further about his comment.

"Well, since last night, I've spent a lot of time thinking about the garage door problem and I believe you've overlooked the light that comes on when the door goes up. It could get some attention, you know, if the humans in the house next door see a garage door in the middle of the night and the light come on when there's no car in the driveway."

Roscoe hadn't thought of that, he hadn't really paid that much attention to the garage door before.

"Plus, my device can only open the door, it can't close it. So…" Sparky couldn't think of anything else to say. He'd stated the problem as he saw it, that was all he could do so he shrugged, signaling he was finished.

"Okay, let's say we move the time up to…" Roscoe scratched out the original time he planned to enter the garage and had started to write another one in when Edgar interrupted.

"Noon would be best," Edgar stood up and paced around the room, looking at the ceiling from time to time hoping to suggest all of this was just coming to him. "The small humans are in school and their parents are at work so nobody's around. I'm telling you, the place is deserted."

"Excellent," Roscoe wrote noon over the time he'd scratched out. "That may cut it kind of close, but you all know what you are supposed to do so let's meet back here a little before noon."

Everyone nodded to the Committee member next to them and some hugged while others shook hands. They sensed this was an historic moment; no Community had ever attempted such a bold plan. The idea that one of their own was going to break into Seed Man's house brought a sense of excitement.

Shortly before noon everyone was assembled under the rose bush at the back of the yard. Everyone gathered around Roscoe while Manny started moving slowly across the yard to take his position beneath the picture window. His role in Roscoe's plan was important but wouldn't come in to play until later, after the feeder rod had been removed from the garage and carried to its usual place in the back yard.

"Okay, Rudy D and I will go in first. Sparky, where do you think we'll find the opener box?"

"I'd guess along the back wall someplace, fairly high." It was a guess too, no one in the Community had ever dared go near the garage much less enter it. If they had, the location of a garage door opener would be the last thing on their mind.

"And you think the door thing you've given me will work okay?"

"Transmitter. It's called a transmitter and yeh, I'm 95% sure it will. Besides, if it doesn't work we haven't lost anything, no ones going in until the door opens. Right?"

"Sure," Roscoe was hoping for a yes or a no but Sparky had made a good point. "Let's check the radio." He held his up to his lips and whispered, "Testing, testing, 1,2,3."

"Ah, Roscoe, you have to push the button down." Sparky spoke into his and pointed to the orange button on the top of the instrument on Roscoe's wrist.

"Oh, right, gotcha." Roscoe pushed the button down a couple of times to make sure he had the idea then looked at the group around him. "Rod team ready?"

Eight squirrels raised their paws.

"Feeder tube teams?"

Eight more paws shot in the air.

"How about the Edelman brothers?"

"They're just coming into the yard now, hold up a minute." Edgar motioned for them to hurry, the operation was about to start.

"Sorry guys we were working out and kind of lost track of time," Rorey explained as they joined the others under the rose bush. "What's going on?"

Roscoe took a moment to go over his plan with them. They nodded as they listened. When he was finished Morey said, "Let's get the show on the road."

"Okay Rudy D, Morey and Rorey, let's go."

Together they sped across the yard and stopped when they reached the stone wall near the garage. They looked around and didn't see any movement on the sidewalk or street.

Roscoe rose up, aimed the opener at the garage door and pushed the button on top.

At first nothing happened. Roscoe started to call for Sparky to join them but stopped when he heard a motor kick on, then watched in amazement as the door started to go up. Roscoe was the first to realize this was a moment for action. "Move it guys," he whispered to the others, "we haven't got all day."

They slipped under the bottom of the door and scanned the walls of the garage. "I got it," Rudy D said and let loose a perfect strike. The acorn bounced off the opener box and the garage door stopped. It had only gone up a foot or so but Roscoe realized they couldn't keep it like that. A garage door partially open would draw too much attention.

He spoke into the wrist radio. "Sparky, how do we get the door to go down? Over."

He let up on the button and waited. "Have Rudy D hit the box again." The radio clicked off then almost immediately came on again. "I think." Sparky's voice sounded funny coming through the little box on his wrist. Roscoe allowed himself a moment to wonder what his voice sounded like on Sparky's end, then snapped out of it and motioned for Rudy D to throw another nut at the box.

Because time was essential, he went into an abbreviated windup and threw another strike. After the door closed he looked around, hoping to find the first two nuts he'd thrown while the garage door light was still on.

Roscoe told the Edelmans to look for the feeder bar. They spotted it, leaning in the corner next to the shelf that held the feeder tubes.

They grabbed the end of the rod and began to work it down the wall. They placed it on the garage floor as close to the location Roscoe had drawn on his sketch as they could.

With that out of the way they climbed back up to the shelf where they'd seen the tubes. Rorey did a forward role, came out of it in a jump and ended with a flip. Rudy D had never seen the brother's work before and stood with his mouth open as they quickly made it up the shelves to the one that held the feeder tubes.

Morey grabbed a tube by the wire loop on the top and pulled it over to the edge of the shelf. He shoved it forward and for just a moment he and the tube were free falling toward the garage floor. Then Rorey grabbed his back legs and held on, holding his brother upside down with the bottom of the feeder tube inches from the floor.

Rudy D and Roscoe ran over and carefully lowered the first tube to the ground while Rorey swung Morey back up to the shelf for the second one.

When it was in position on the garage floor next to the first one, the Edelmans flipped to the ground and landed without making a sound.

"Fantastic," was all Rudy D could say.

Roscoe got on the radio. "Sparky, send the feeder rod and tube teams in. We're ready. Tell them to knock twice when they're in position." He heard Sparky say, "Roger that good buddy." Before he signed off Roscoe could hear Marvin and Jules giggling in the background.

Roscoe's eyes had gradually grown accustomed to the darkness of the garage. While he waited for the feeder rod team to knock on the door he took a moment to look around. He saw a rake, lawn mower, a second car and wondered why Seed Man needed all this stuff. He thought about his nest; nothing there but a few seeds tucked away for a rainy day and some straw to cover up with at night. He glanced at the shelves against the back wall covered with boxes and cans of paint. He was about to turn back to the garage door when he spotted a full, unopened bag of seeds on the top shelf.

He was thinking so intently about the bag of seeds he almost missed the two light taps on the door. He aimed the opener toward the door opener at the back wall and pushed the red button. The door went up a foot and stopped when Rudy D bounced another acorn off the opener.

Immediately the three teams of squirrels darted in and went about their business; grabbing the items off the floor and taking them to a pre-arranged spot in the back yard. When they got there, they slipped the feeder tubes over the arms on the feeder rod and lifted the whole apparatus up. They held it in place while Manny climbed part way up and let his weight push the feeder rod into the ground.

When the garage floor was clear, Rudy D was about to bounce another acorn off the opener just before the four of them made their exit under the door as it closed. At least, that was the way Roscoe's plan was supposed to work, he'd called it their, *exit strategy*.

"Close the door Rudy D, and the rest of you stay put for a minute."

Rudy D gave Roscoe a funny look but went ahead with his throw, hitting the box and lowering the door.

"What's up," Rorey asked as the door banged shut.

"That." He looked where Roscoe was pointing and saw the seed bag only three shelves above the ground.

"Let's go man, we've done our job. If we hang around and mess with that we're just asking for trouble." Rudy D started to reach for the opener in Roscoe's paw.

"Hold on a minute," Morey spoke slowly, like he was trying to work out a plan.

Roscoe spoke into his radio. "Sparky, is the feeder up?"

Sparky's voice came back, "We're just about there. Manny's on the pole and it's going down slowly but it is going down. Some of the others have climbed on trying to add a little more weight. Hold it one of them just waved." There was a break as Sparky stepped away to check on the progress of the feeder then he was back. "Okay, it's in place. What's going on? You were supposed to be out of there by now."

"Right, I hear you but ah, something's come up. Get the teams together and wait until you hear from me. We've just hit the mother lode." Sparky could hear the excitement in Roscoe's voice before the radio clicked off.

Inside the garage the Edelmans were already on the shelf and walking around on top of the bag of seeds.

"I think if the four of us get between the bag and the wall we could shove it enough to get it to the floor," Morey explained as he climbed behind the bag and gave it a push.

"Then I call the teams back in, they whisk it away to a hiding place in the back yard." Roscoe took the idea a step further.

"Then we close the door and were out of here." Rorey added the final detail to the plan.

"I'm telling you guys this is a mistake. We've done what he came to do, let's go." Rudy D didn't like tense situations, especially ones that involved a dark room where the only way out is under a door that at the moment was closed.

"You lose three to one, Rudy D. Hop up here and help push." Morey was already in position; his back was against the wall and his feet pushing on the bag. The others joined him.

They'd moved the bag a few inches when they froze. The little motor that caused the garage door to open clicked on and the door started up.

Rudy D stood and fired a strike, stopping it from going any higher.

Roscoe whispered into the radio, "What's going on Sparky?"

"Oh, It was me Roscoe, Marvin here. I, ah, well, hit the button by mistake. Sorry."

The four inside finally exhaled and laughed. Rudy D flipped another acorn at the opener box and the door closed.

They worked some more, moving the bag enough so it hung half way off the shelf.

"Guy's. I don't think this is a good idea. I'm afraid when the bag drops..." Rudy D was standing on the edge of the shelf, looking down.

"We'll take it from here." Rorey and Morey spoke as they started into a forward roll toward the bag. They sprang up when their feet touched the surface of the shelf, flipped in the air and hit the bag with all the force they could muster.

Nothing happened for a moment, then the bag slowly went over the edge. It hit the floor with a smack that was followed by a rip as the sack split open and its contents slid across the garage floor.

The four of them stood on the edge of the shelf and listened as Rudy D finished what he was saying, "...it will break."

While they gathered around the broken bag, trying to figure out their next move, the motor in the door opener over their heads clicked on again.

"Marvin, if is this another mistake of yours, so help me." Roscoe let up on the transmitter button.

The door continued to go up and at the same time Roscoe heard Sparky say, "They're home."

When the garage door was half way up, Roscoe could see the head lights of Seed Man's car.

The four squirrels scrambled up the shelving and crammed themselves behind a box on the top shelf.

The car pulled halfway into the garage and stopped when Seed Man saw the bag of seeds on the ground.

He shut off the car's engine and got out.

Roscoe heard Sweetheart ask what was wrong. He said something she couldn't understand and she told him he'd mumbled through their whole vacation and she was tired of it. If he had something to say why didn't he just he just come out and say it.

He opened the trunk of the car, removed two suitcases and carried them into the house.

Sweetheart got out on her side and followed him. She carried a box of some kind with her. Roscoe could hear seeds crunching beneath her shoes as she made her way across the garage floor.

After she left and it was quiet in the garage again.

The four members of the feeder recovery team peeked from behind the boxes and saw the coast was clear. They dropped to the garage floor and headed out through the open door.

Roscoe stopped when he got outside, his eyes fixed on the broken bag of seeds on the garage floor. "So close," he mumbled. Rudy D grabbed his elbow and gave it a tug. "Let it go Roscoe," he whispered. "Sometimes you just have to let things go."

Roscoe sighed, took a last look at the seeds spread across the floor and joined the others running across the yard. He glanced toward the area near the picture window at the back of the house. The feeder rod looked straight and secure, the two empty feeder tubes hung from the hooks. At least they'd accomplished something, he thought. This time his plan hadn't been a complete failure.

By late afternoon everyone in the community had heard of the daring raid into Seed Man's garage and how Roscoe and his teammates had put up the feeder. They gathered in little clusters in the tall grass at the edge of the yard and talked. Eventually they grew silent, waiting to see if the second part of Roscoe's plan would work as well as the first.

Seed Man had been busy taking things out of his car and carrying them into the house. There was a period of time when no one could account for him, someone said they thought they saw him sweeping up the seeds in the garage, but it was just a guess.

Everyone in the community watched the big picture window for some sign of him. They hoped he was getting ready to bring seeds to the feeder but they knew there was no guarantee he would.

Finally, he showed up with a cup of coffee in one hand and a cookie in the other. Although they couldn't hear any sounds from the house they could see Sweetheart waving her arms and her mouth moving.

The crowd in the tall grass watched as Seed Man scanned the yard, checking on how much the grass had grown while he was gone and looking to see if anything was coming up in his garden. His gaze stopped when it came to the feeder. They could tell he was trying to remember if he had taken the feeder down before he left or not. He turned his head slightly, hoping that might help him think a little better.

Then he disappeared from the window.

The entire community sighed with disappointment. They had seen nothing in his look that suggested he was thinking,

"Oh no, the feeders empty. I'd better do something about it or those poor squirrels will starve." He'd been drinking from his cup and eating a cookie one minute and was gone the next.

Most of them turned around to head back to their nests thinking maybe he'd fill the feeder in the morning while others weren't as optimistic.

They stopped when the heard the sound of the garage door go up. Seed Man rounded the corner and started across the yard carrying a brown bag. He filled the feeder tubes one at a time and turned to go back to the garage.

A cheer went up from the little Community gathered at the edge of the yard. As different as they were in age and interest, Edgar and Roscoe hugged and patted each other on the back. Roscoe could hear him say, "Well done my boy. Well done," between sobs of joy.

Morey crouched and formed a step with his paws and when Rorey stepped into it, Morey straightened up and sent him high in the air.

Sparky smiled. He required no thanks, just knowing the two devices he'd made worked was good enough for him.

Seed Man stopped and looked around. He thought he'd heard something. The yard grew quiet and eventually he figured he'd been mistaken. He continued on to the garage and closed the door.

The silence that remained from having almost been caught was broken by Marvin's voice.

"Ah, guys, lets not be bashful. Dinner is served." He took off for the feeder slightly ahead of the Flying Edelman's.

CHAPTER 5
A Plan Reversed

"There it is!" Roscoe stood in his nest in the top of the elm at the back of Seed Man's yard, pointing at the base of the feeder. "There. It. Is!" he repeated emphasizing each word .

Marvin, who had been sleeping on a branch next to Roscoe woke up and looked around thinking he was about to be attacked. He saw Roscoe leaning forward and pointing. "I knew it," Roscoe said excitedly. "I told you it would happen and its happened."

Marvin was having trouble figuring out what was going on, this wasn't the normal, easy going Roscoe he'd grown up with. That Roscoe would never thinking of scaring a friend who was in the middle of a much needed nap half out of his wits by yelling and pointing at things. And he would never, ever, stand in his nest.

"What are you talking about Roscoe?" Marvin rubbed his eyes and stretched.

"Look," was all Roscoe said and pointed to the squirrel feeder.

"I don't see any…" Marvin stopped in the middle of his sentence, "Well I'll be."

He saw what had caused his friend to get so excited, a full bag of seeds was leaning against the feeder pole.

They scrambled down the side of the tree and crept to the rose bush at the edge of the yard. Marvin had a hard time keeping up with Roscoe who, in his hurry to check things out, seemed to have shifted into a higher gear. They squeezed under the bush and squatted down while they made a quick survey of the yard; Seed Man was nowhere in sight and the bag was still leaning against the pole.

Roscoe looked at the bag and noticed a plastic cord had been tied around the top, put there he assumed, to keep the seeds from spilling out if the bag fell over.

"Sweet," Marvin heard Roscoe whisper. Then in a louder voice he spoke to Marvin but kept his eyes on the seed bag. "Mobilize the seed bag team, and step on it. We may not have a lot of time."

Marvin started to protest, to advise Roscoe to slow down and think about what he was doing but realized it would be useless to say anything because he had that look.

Pretty soon the twenty-four squirrels who made up the seed bag team were gathered around the rose bush. They were all talking at once. Some wanted to know what was going on while others said, "This had better be good, you can only cry seeds so many times." They all knew the story of the young squirrel who cried, "Seeds," because he thought it was fun to watch everyone run around the yard looking for them. Roscoe couldn't remember the point of the story but he knew who ever said it was right, this time his plan had to work.

"Send Jules out," Roscoe gave the command and Jules started

across the yard as if he had all day to get to the feeder and not a care in the world. This would be the test. If Jules could make it to the feeder, climb up, eat a few seeds and return without something happening to him, it would show the coast was clear and the bag of seeds was his.

Jules walked slowly away from the feeder. "Sorry I took so long," he explained, "but I thought I'd take a look around once I was up there." He pointed to the top of the feeder. "Then I started nibbling on the seeds and…" Roscoe knew how much Jules liked to eat so he nodded and said he understood.

"Follow me guys." Roscoe took off across the yard with the Seed bag team close behind. When they got to the base of the feeder, they spread themselves evenly around the bag like they had practiced and grabbed the side in front of them. Roscoe gave the command to lift and the bag slowly rose off the ground.

He ran around in front of them, checked to make sure the path to the staging area was clear and unobstructed. Then, in a dramatic gesture, he leaned forward, stuck out his right arm and said, "Head 'um up and move 'um out."

The bag started moving, floating inches above the ground. Roscoe kept his pose, pointing to the edge of the yard, as the bag moved past him.

There was a blinding flash. No one was expecting it. The seed bag team dropped the bag and staggered around the yard, temporarily blinded. When they finally regained their sight, they took off for the side of the yard nearest them.

Roscoe couldn't figure out what happened. Everything was going so well, the bag was moving, the members of the seed bag team were fresh and eager.

Then there was the flash.

As his vision began to return he saw Seed Man wriggle out

The Squirrel Chronicles: Book One

from under the deck holding a small gray box in his hand.

He stood up and gave a squeal of excitement. "Sweetheart," he called to his wife inside the house, "I got it. I got the picture. This one's going to win first place for sure."

Roscoe looked at the big picture window at the back of the house and saw Sweetheart clapping her hands and smiling.

Seed Man started to jog across the yard toward the garage then suddenly stopped and returned to the feeder. He picked up the seed bag and held it in the air. He did a little dance in a circle and said, "The best part is there's only paper inside, no seeds at all," He held the bag up for Sweetheart to see. She nodded yes and blew him a kiss. He laughed, grabbed the air kiss and danced his way across the yard until he disappeared around the corner of the house.

Roscoe couldn't move. His legs felt like they were made of lead and he was still dizzy from the flash. Gradually it dawned on him that he had been fooled by the, *"Fake Seed Bag Sitting Out In the Open,"* trick, the first example they use on opening day of seed school.

He didn't know how he could have been so dumb.

He felt someone tug on his arm. "Shake it off buddy." Marvin pulled some more and Roscoe didn't fight it, he allowed himself to be led to the safety of the shrubbery.

The worst thing for him though was the laughter from the members of the Community as he made his way to his tree and climbed to his nest. It was much worse than the screeching he'd received from the members of the Committee to Protect Neighborhood Resources after a previous failed attempt. For him the laughter from his friends was the hardest to take.

He spent a restless night reliving every wrong move he'd ever made in his life. As a result, he woke the next morning feeling worse than when he'd gone to bed. He rolled over and lay on his side, staring into the distance, not really focusing on anything.

"Good morning Roscoe," a voice came from a branch in front of him. Roscoe looked closer and tried to focus but couldn't. The sun was behind whoever was speaking and he wasn't able to make out any features but unfortunately he recognized the voice.

"Is that you Sid?" He spoke to the shape in front of him.

"Right you are Roscoe. It is I." Sid answered and decided the tactic of using the sun behind him to confuse Roscoe wasn't working. He followed the branch he was on to the trunk of the tree then took another one that put him even with Roscoe's nest.

"You don't believe in reading signs then?" Roscoe moved so he was facing away from his guest.

"Oh yes. The reading of signs is what I do Roscoe. But that could have a double meaning couldn't it?" Sid paused. Long pauses were part of his counseling technique. He'd started out in the same seed school class as Roscoe but after graduation went away to study. He'd written a groundbreaking book about squirrel Communities and was recognized as an expert trauma counselor. He was usually brought in when a Community member had a close call with a dog or a small human with a BB gun.

His fur was always neat and well combed. He was the only one in the Community who used safflower oil to slick down the fur around his face.

"If I might make one correction to the aforementioned sign Roscoe, StayAway is two words not one." Sid smiled. "Stay. Away. Two words."

"Either way though, stay away means stay away." Roscoe

The Squirrel Chronicles: Book One

knew word would quickly spread through the Community that Sid had paid him a visit adding to his humiliation.

"I see." Sid wrote something on a pad he held in his paw. "But sometimes I have found the sign that says, *Stay Away*, is actually saying, *Help me!* Hmmm?" Humming at precise moments was also part of his technique. "What do you think about that Roscoe?"

"In this case, StayAway means exactly what it says, Stay Away, nothing more, nothing less. I hope that doesn't mess up one of your little theories." Roscoe kept his back to him. He was afraid if he rolled over and looked at him he'd be tempted to push him off the limb he was sitting on.

"About your fascination with, what is it?" Roscoe could hear pages turning in his notepad. "Ah, here we are, bags of seeds. Would you care to share your feelings on that subject?"

"No."

"Hmmm. I remember growing up with a happy, fun loving squirrel who was curious about life, but back then weren't we all?" Sid waited a moment before continuing. "Roscoe, where did that young squirrel go? We don't grow too old to play you know, we grow old because we don't play. Hmmm."

"If you're referring to me, I'm still here, just a little disillusioned at the moment." Roscoe didn't like the direction the discussion was taking, he was talking way too much. He knew the best strategy when Sid was around was to keep quiet and he'd eventually go away. "And, in case you haven't noticed, I'm not the only one who's grown up."

Sid smiled. Things were going better than he'd expected. He was concerned by the angry tone in Roscoe's voice but knew that had to come out before there was any hope that healing could take place.

"Well," Sid glanced at the position of the sun, "looks like our time is up for today. Hmmm? What say we get together tomorrow? How about," he thumbed through the pages of his planner, "noonish?" He waited but got nothing from Roscoe. "Until then, I'd like you to be thinking about your future Roscoe. Will it be spent here in your nest, an outcast, living alone, isolated from everything you hold dear without a sole to talk to or will it be in the company of friends laughing and frolicking around the feeder?"

Roscoe groaned.

"Will you think about that Roscoe?"

"I'll try to work it in to my schedule," Roscoe grunted.

"Excellent, that's all I can ask." Roscoe could hear him humming as he made his way down the tree.

"Good grief," Roscoe muttered and burrowed further into his nest.

"Psst," Marvin had taken Sid's place on the limb.

"Sid, I swear if you don't…" Roscoe rolled over and discovered It was Marvin not Sid who was trying to get his attention.

"Oh, sorry Marvin, I thought…"

"Sure, no problem Roscoe, but ah…" He made a gesture with his head indicating Roscoe should look over the side of his nest.

"What is it Marvin? Can't you just tell me? I'm not really in the mood for guessing games." After his encounter with Sid, Roscoe decided that from now on he'd just say what was on his mind and not beat around the bush.

Marvin said, "It's…" and made the gesture with his head again.

Roscoe sighed, moved to the edge of his nest and looked down. He saw the huge back and tiny head of Manny waiting at the base of his tree.

"Okay, okay," he said as he pulled himself out of his nest and climbed down.

"What's up Manny?" Rocoe felt like a dwarf standing next to him.

"The way I see it Rosc," Manny's husky voice was barely above a whisper. "Someone hits me, I hit them back. You see what I'm saying?"

After delivering his message Manny turned and waddled away, his huge body rolling from side to side.

"When was I hit Manny?" Roscoe stood by the tree, his paws in the air, confused by the message. "Who am I supposed to hit?" He watched until Manny turned a corner and was out of sight.

Roscoe tore the *StayAway* sign from the trunk of his tree since it didn't seem to be doing any good. He headed to his nest and assumed his thinking position; stomach pressed against the floor and his chin resting on the edge. He couldn't stop thinking about why Manny would leave his nest, which he seldom did, come all the way over to his tree and say something that made absolutely no sense. He was wishing Manny had been a little more talkative when he heard something hit the top of his tree.

"Hey. Watch out. Heads up. Whoa. Yipes." Words tumbled from the branches over Roscoe's head. The words were followed by the body of Wilbur, a member of the Community of Abner, grabbing at tree limbs as he fell toward Roscoe. He snagged a solid branch and stopped inches before they collided.

"Ah, how you doing Roscoe?" Wilbur hung by one arm for a moment then let go and dropped in the nest next to him.

Everyone in the Community knew Wilbur was not his real name but at some point they started calling him that. The name change came shortly after he was big enough to climb out of the family nest; he couldn't stop thinking about flying. When he wasn't asking other member's their opinion on the subject, or checking out books from the Community library, he was dropping things from his nest and studying the flight pattern as they floated to the ground.

"Wilbur what are you doing here?" Roscoe was having trouble shifting mental gears from thinking about hitting something back that hits you to having a squirrel wearing a leather aviators cap standing next to him.

"Well, to tell you the truth, I'm not sure. I took off from that oak tree over there and must have nicked a branch or something. But, like they say, no harm no foul. I'll just bail out of here and reexamine my flight path."

Roscoe looked to see which tree he was talking about. He spotted one but was sure that couldn't be, it was at least 30 feet away. On his best day, he could only make an 8 or 10 foot jump.

He pointed and asked, "Are you talking about that tree over there?"

Wilbur looked. "Yep, that's the one. How I ended up over here I'll never know. Maybe the wind pushed me…" He stared at the edge of the nest for a moment trying to figure out what had gone wrong. He looked up, blinked and apologized again. "Sorry for the interruption."

Wilbur was about to climb out of the nest when Roscoe had one of those flashes of inspiration that seldom come to other squirrels but seem to pay him regular visits.

"Hold up Wilbur, I was wondering if you're busy tomorrow afternoon." Roscoe wasn't actually looking at Wilbur but at a spot several feet above his head. He was waiting for the last piece of a plan to fall in place. When it did, he lowered his gaze, studied Wilbur for a second and smiled.

"Sure, it's not like I have to check my calendar or anything. What do you have in mind?" He stepped back into the nest as Roscoe with words and gestures explained his plan.

"Cool," Wilbur said when he finished. Then he left the nest and headed back to the oak tree to see if he couldn't nail the flight he'd been working on before he ran out of daylight.

Roscoe got the feeling he gets when a, "can't miss," plan comes together in his mind. He had a few things to do before he could relax but for him, getting the idea was the hard part, the rest was just working out the details. He scurried down the tree and headed for Sid's office.

"What a surprise to see you Roscoe. The feeling I had about our last session was you had a lot of resentment toward me." Sid was sitting on a couch in his small but nicely decorated office. A jar of nuts was on the edge of his desk next to his notepad. He'd just finished with a client when Roscoe knocked on the door.

"You probably got that one right Sid. I was frustrated after coming so close to reaching my goal. Then there was the flash and well, you know." Roscoe answered doing his best to project the picture of a young squirrel who'd seen the error of his ways.

"Hmmm." Sid hummed and flipped through the pages of his notepad, going back to their earlier session. "So, you feel our talk this morning was helpful?"

"Almost helpful Sid. Very close to being helpful might describe it better." Roscoe knew he was walking a fine line giving Sid just enough encouragement to keep him interested but conveying there was more work to be done.

"Hmmm. Personal reflection is a healthy step forward Roscoe." Sid pulled his appointment scheduler across his desk and studied it. "I have an opening next Tues…"

Roscoe shook his head. "Sid, to tell you the truth I'm

desperate. I keep getting this urge to nab seed bags, coming up with crazy schemes that couldn't possibly work and could possibly endanger the lives of others in the Community." He wrung his paws and paced back and forth like a patient on the edge.

Sid hesitated. Something was not quite right here but he couldn't put his paw on what it was. "Did you have something in mind? A time to…"

Roscoe interrupted again. "As a matter of fact I thought, now this is just me talking, someone without your training but, well, what if we met the problem head on?"

"Hmmm. Head on like…?"

"Have a session at the feeder which is, as I'm sure you have already figured out, at the heart of my problem." Roscoe wrinkled his brow and gave his most plaintiff look; it was one that had always worked on his mother.

"At the feeder you say? Hmmm." Sid tapped the side of the notepad with a pencil. The beginning of a technical paper formed in his mind. *Meeting Your Problem Head On by Dr. Sidney*, was the working title he'd selected and he could hear the applause of his peers who were overwhelmed by his breakthrough work.

"Yes. Where better to beat back the cause of my temptation than at the source?" Roscoe tried to phrase things so they sounded like he was reflecting what Sid had said.

"Do you ah, hmmm, have a time in mind for this meeting?"

"I was thinking, tomorrow afternoon, say, oh, around four?" Roscoe thought he could have everything in place by then. Besides, he knew that was about the time Seed Man came out to start his bar-b-quer.

Sid frowned when he saw he already had a four o'clock

appointment scheduled for that time. He put his paws behind his back and paced in a small circle. Which was more important, he wondered, taking part in a ground breaking new therapy that could revolutionize methods of treatment for thousands of squirrels facing the same fixation as Roscoe or help Edgar work through his fear of heights?

"I can reschedule." He said quickly and made a note on the corner of his pad to find a new time for Edgar.

"Wonderful," Roscoe did his best to sound grateful as he walked to the door. "You know, it's funny, I actually feel better already." He closed the door before Sid could say anything, he had more work to do and very little time to do it in.

He stood under Manny's nest and shouted instructions but wasn't sure if he was listening. The key phrase he'd used several times was, "It's about hitting back." After a long pause he heard Manny's familiar gruff voice mumble, "Gotcha," so he knew that part of the plan was taken care of.

He made a check mark on his to do list next to Manny's name. There were four names on the list, Sid, Wilbur, Manny and Sparky and by the end of the day each name had a check mark beside it except Sparky's.

Sparky is, the Community technical genius and when Roscoe explained his role in what he was calling *Operation Strike Back*. His usual, "No problem," helped him relax, it was good to have people on the team he knew he could count on.

"All that's left is to pick up a couple of pieces of furniture and I'm set," he said as he sat in his nest and went over his notes. Things were coming together and try as he might, he couldn't see a flaw in the plan. He knew from experience the best ideas come like this, not studied or planned but spontaneous. It started with a huge mistake on his part, was followed by a visit by Sid, then a wayward fly over by Wilbur-you can't plan all that, but you can use it.

The next afternoon on the way to the feeder he saw Manny's huge body rocking from side to side, headed for his assigned place.

As he got closer to Seed Man's yard he saw Sparky standing in front of an easel. He was using a pointer to identify a round tube inside a gray box. The two young squirrels sitting in front of him nodded their heads and told him they understood what they were supposed to do.

After a quick glance at the rose bush where the three members of the furniture team stood, Roscoe hopped out to the feeder.

He knew he was a little early when he got to the base of the feeder pole but better early than late he told himself. He hoped he didn't appear too eager and scare Sid off. On his way across the yard he'd scanned the back of the house, looking for some sign of Seed Man but hadn't seen any.

He lay down on the small couch the furniture team had moved from Sid's office and placed near the feeder pole.

He was just about to doze off when he heard Sid's voice. "What's going on Roscoe? Why did you bring my sofa and chair out here?" There was a touch of anger in his usual calm voice, he didn't like others moving his furniture around with out asking him first.

"Sorry, Sid. I was just trying to recreate the feel of your office. I thought it would be helpful for both of us. For you actually. I know your office is kind of like your work shop." Roscoe was pleased with the way that came out and was pretty sure Sid bought it.

"Hmmm. A little unusual but then again this is a ground

breaking procedure so I'll give it a try." Sid sat down in his chair and flipped through his notebook looking for a clean piece of paper.

"I think it started when I was little, this ah, need to do something out of the ordinary," Roscoe began.

Sid found a brand new, freshly sharpened pencil on the arm of his chair and wrote down Roscoe's comments, humming quietly whenever he heard something he thought was important.

Roscoe talked and glanced at the door by the deck wondering why it was taking Seed Man so long to come out. He hoped this was not one of those rare Saturday afternoons when he and Sweetheart went out to eat. He led Sid through his formative years, shared his daily schedule with him while occasionally glancing at the back door.

"Have you always had that?" Sid interrupted him.

"What?"

"The twitch in your eye, the inability to stay focused on something for any length of time?" Sid wrote on his notepad as he spoke.

"It's interesting you mention that Sid." Roscoe wanted to extend the session as long as he could so he launched into an explanation of how he'd acquired the twitch.

It wasn't until he was starting to analyze each of his previous failures at getting the bag of seeds that Roscoe saw Seed Man approach the patio door from inside the house. He held a bag of charcoal in one hand and a plate of hamburgers in the other while attempting to open the sliding door with his elbow.

About the time Roscoe spotted Seed Man, Seed Man spotted Roscoe. He stood motionless at the door, trying to figure out what to do. Then he slowly backed away and Roscoe's heart sank. We lost him, he thought. Without Seed Man there would be no solution to the puzzle that had haunted him every since the flash from the gray box in his hand the day before. He tried to keep the disappointment out of his voice.

All that was going on in his mind while he droned on about the seed bag splitting open or Manny bending the feeder pole down. Sid's chair had been placed so he was facing away from the deck and had no idea Seed Man had come to the door and then gone.

Roscoe saw movement at the corner of the house and told himself to relax as he watched Seed Man work his way across the yard, trying to get as close as possible to the strange scene at the base of the feeder to take his picture. The first, tentative title he'd chosen was, *The Doctor Is In.*

Sid stopped writing, his survival instincts kicking in. Roscoe shifted from describing failed seed heists to unusual dreams he'd had that might be at the root of his problem. Sid hung for a second between the warning signs that told him to flee and the chance to unravel the meaning of Roscoe's dreams.

Unraveling dreams won and Sid flipped to a new page in his book. "Did you say it was raining that night or that you thought it was raining?"

Seed Man got as close as he could and carefully brought the camera up, trying to frame the perfect shot. While he focused on the scene in front of him, Manny waddled out from under the deck and quietly took his place behind him.

Seemingly out of nowhere, Seed Man saw a squirrel wearing a leather cap sailing through the air, coming straight at him. He stepped back to protect himself and lost his balance as he tripped over Manny. He dropped the camera and it opened up as it bounced on the ground exposing the film inside.

As soon as the camera came to rest the two squirrels Roscoe had seen with Sparky, broke from the rose bush and ran straight for it. Seed Man watched in amazement as one squirrel held the camera steady while the other removed the film. They both took off for the edge of the yard carrying the canister of film between them.

Manny crawled under the deck, wiggled out the other side and headed back to his nest. He smiled as he thought about the promise Roscoe had made to have a cup of seeds delivered to his nest every morning for the next week.

In the confusion, Sid leapt from his chair and took off for the safety of the back of the yard. When he was almost to the tall grass he realized he'd left his notebook at the feeder and raced back to get it.

Roscoe lifted Sid's small leather chair and carried it across the yard. The members of the furniture team grabbed the couch and followed close behind him.

Seed Man sat on the ground propped up on his elbows. "They'll never believe this," he repeated several times. He started to call Sweetheart and tell her what had happened, but realized she probably wouldn't believe it either. Besides it was over now, there was nothing left for her to see. He finally decided if someone had told him what he had just experienced he wouldn't believed it either. He found his camera, turned over on its side; he knew the film was missing. He picked it up, brushed off the seat of his pants and shrugged; "There'll be other shots to take," he said quietly. He turned toward the back of the yard and hollered into the trees, "There'll be other shots to take, you can count on it."

He stomped across the yard growing angrier as he remembered the picture he'd taken they day before of the twenty four squirrels carrying the fake bag of seeds was on that role of film they'd taken.

Roscoe had the members of the strike back team huddled around him. He could account for the furniture movers and the film carriers. He knew Sid would eventually make it back to his office, not sure if Roscoe meant it when he stood up and shouted, "You've done it, I'm cured."

He'd seen Manny waddling back to his nest but couldn't account for Wilbur?

"Wilbur?" He asked in a whisper as he made his way across the back yard. "Wilbur, where are you?"

"Up here Roscoe," Wilbur's voice carried to the ground. Roscoe looked up and saw him hanging from the top of the feeder pole by his front paws. "I didn't account for the updraft around the feeder or I'd been okay."

He dropped to the ground next to Roscoe.

"Mission accomplished Wilbur." Roscoe put an arm around his shoulder. "You couldn't have done any better."

There was a sudden flash and everything went white around them. When their vision began to clear they took off in a dead run for the tall grass.

When they got to a safe place, Wilbur spun around and asked, "What was that?"

Roscoe looked at the deck and saw Seed Man doing a little dance, shuffling his feet back and forth and pumping his arms in the air.

He yelled in their direction, "I told you, you don't mess with Harold Finebender and get away with it."

He held the gray box in his hand. "No sir-e-bob. Know this, when you mess with Harold Finebender you better bring your lunch because you're in for a long day."

The Squirrel Chronicles: Book One

Roscoe stood for a moment and shook his head in disbelief. He was about to ask himself if he was doomed for failure when he heard Wilbur ask, "Did he say something about lunch?"

He looked at the feeder and then back at Wilbur. "Why not?" He said, "At least we won't go home hungry."

CHAPTER 6

A Field of Seeds

It was tucked between two flowering shrubs. The top of the bag was open and a few seeds had spilled out and were lying on the ground. Roscoe could see the printing on the bag that said it weighed 10 pounds. The sky was blue and the best part was, there was no one else around. At a time like this you don't ask what a 10 pound bag of seeds is doing in an open field between flowering shrubs.

You go for it.

He reached for the bag but something prevented his arm from moving. He pulled but couldn't seem to make any progress.

Someone called his name.

"Roscoe."

The seed bag faded. Blooms dropped from the bushes. The tug became more forceful and clouds moved in marring the perfect sky.

"Roscoe, wake up." The voice, closer now, called again.

He opened his eyes and found the face of Edgar, Chairman of the Committee for the Protection of Neighborhood Resources inches from his. Out of the corner of his eye he saw the rest of the Committee spaced evenly around the edge of his nest.

"Good. You're awake." Edgar leaned back, unaware he'd interrupted Roscoe's favorite dream.

"What time is it anyway?" Roscoe asked. He closed his eyes for a moment to let his head clear. Maybe this was a dream and the other, running across an open field toward a bag of seeds was real.

He opened his eyes again and knew from the grim look on the faces of those around him, it wasn't.

"I deeply apologize for this unfortunate interruption of *your personal time* but we have an emergency on our hands that can't wait until later in the morning when it would be *more convenient for you*." Sarcasm dripped from each of Edgar's words.

Roscoe could tell by the half-light that filtered through the tree branches that it was still early in the morning, at least it was for him.

"An emergency you say?" He sat up to clear his thoughts as the last fragment of the dream zipped out of sight. He knew there was no way he could bring it back. There had been emergencies before but the Committee had always stopped him when he was going someplace or waited for him at the bottom of his tree until he had a chance to wake up. It was rare for Edgar to get this far off the ground because of his fear of heights.

"Of the most dire type Roscoe, the most dire type indeed." Normally Edgar paced back and forth when he talked but given the distance from the ground and the narrowness of the limb he was standing on, he choose to rock from side to side instead.

Roscoe heard the members of the Committee repeat the word, "Dire."

"There's a dog, my granddaughter Penny Sue, the feeder, she was…" Edgar couldn't go on, he'd become too emotional. His shoulders shook as he struggled to keep himself under control.

Darin, a member of the Committee and one of Roscoe's staunchest supporters, stepped forward. "His granddaughter Penny Sue left the nest early this morning to go to the feeder and…"

"She's a beautiful, precious little girl, Roscoe. Absolutely precious." Edgar couldn't help interrupting. He realized he was preventing Darin from completing the story, so he apologized and gestured with his paw for him to continue.

"It appears she made it to the feeder okay but it looks like Sweetheart has come up with a dog from someplace and…"

Edgar interrupted again feeling Darin's story telling ability wasn't up to the drama of the event. "And that ferocious beast won't let my dear, sweet, precious, Penny Sue get down." His voice dropped to almost a whisper, "I don't know how much longer she can hold on."

Roscoe was trying to picture Penny Sue but couldn't come up with anyone. Edgar had said she was his granddaughter but he knew she wasn't from the Community of Abner so he reasoned she must be visiting from another one. Then it came to him. When he was very young, barely out of the nest, he'd witnessed a Community banishment. A member named Manfred had broken a long standing rule and had fallen in love with a girl named Doreen from another Community.

He'd watched the members of the Committee form two lines facing each other while Manfred endured their silence as he walked between them. He remembered seeing an attractive girl standing at the end of the line. They were both weeping as Manfred embraced her, took one last look at his old Community and walked away to join hers.

The Squirrel Chronicles: Book One

It finally dawned on him, Penny Sue must be Manfred's daughter and that meant that Manfred was Edgar's son, he'd never made the connection.

Edgar interrupted his thinking. "You're our only hope of rescuing her before some tragic…" He couldn't continue. He pressed his paws against his face trying to stop the tears that rolled down his cheeks as he pictured what would happened to his beloved Penny Sue if she fell from the feeder.

He looked at Roscoe but didn't need to say anything, his look said it all.

"A ferocious dog you say?" Roscoe was out of his nest and headed down the tree. He cut across the back of Seed Man's yard and took his place behind the tree limb that dips down and almost touches the ground.

The rest of the Committee caught up with him and crowded around.

"Any ideas yet?" Edgar asked, hope filling each word.

"Has anyone seen Skipper?" Roscoe asked. His question was meant as an inquiry but in the hands of the Committee it became a demand. He heard some one say, "Get Skipper and step on it."

Skipper is, paws down, the fastest squirrel in the Community. In local races he'd cross the finish line and lay down with his head propped up on one paw. Usually he'd find a long blade of grass and chew on it like he'd been there a long time when his closest competitor finished, gasping for breath.

Word of his speed had spread through other neighborhoods and occasionally a challenger would show up to take him on but there'd never been a real threat

Roscoe heard some commotion behind him and the sound of squirrels stepping aside. "You looking for me Rosc?"

Skipper was lean and fit looking. "I was doing some speed

work when they said you wanted to see me. What's up?"

Roscoe turned him toward Seed Man's house and pointed to the feeder.

Skipper saw the dog crouched at the base of the feeder and asked, "What'd you have in mind?"

"This is just a first thought but if you could distract the dog long enough I think I can get Penny Sue off the feeder and out of the yard over there." He pointed to a large bush at the corner of the house."

"Wow." Skipper saw Penny Sue for the first time fighting to keep her balance on the thin rod at the top the feeder. "She is cute. Friend of yours?"

Edgar stepped between them. "She's my only granddaughter Skipper. My only precious…" Seeing her clinging to the feeder and the dog waiting patiently for her to fall

was too much for him.

"She needs our help Skipper, let's see what you can do." Roscoe gave him a little shove and sent him into the yard toward the dog.

Skipper was confident of his speed and loved to have it challenged. He made a few short hops toward the feeder and saw the dog's eyes flick his way then return to the struggling Penny Sue.

Skipper yelped like he'd twisted his ankle when he landed. He continued toward the feeder, limping badly.

"Oh that's just great, he hurt himself," Roscoe heard Edgar moan. "You better come up with another plan Roscoe, this one isn't going to work."

"He's faking it, Edgar. He's trying to make it look like he's an easy catch." It was obvious to Roscoe Edgar was too emotionally involved to be able to see things clearly. He was thinking of

The Squirrel Chronicles: Book One

asking him to wait in the Committee meeting room until the rescue effort was over.

The dog's eyes flicked Skipper's way again and he wagged his tail.

Skipper limped a little closer, acting like he was unaware of the dogs presence.

The dog stood with his tail wagging and his head pointed toward Skipper. "He's big," Roscoe muttered to himself. "Edgar got that part right."

A low growl came from deep inside the dog's chest. He lifted his front paw like he was about to move forward.

"Not too close Skipper," Roscoe whispered, "leave yourself a way out."

Just as the dog was about to take off after Skipper, Roscoe heard a knock on the big picture window at the back of the house. He saw Sweetheart, wearing a pale blue housecoat and a green scarf pulled over the curlers in her hair trying to get the dogs attention.

The dog sat down and resumed his position looking up at Penny Sue.

Sweetheart decided to stay at the window and keep an eye on the dog.

Skipper moved closer and laid down on the ground. He slowly rolled over on his back, making himself completely defenseless.

The dog struggled with what to do. He stood. His head swiveled from Skipper to Sweetheart then back to Skipper.

He whined.

But he knew who filled his food bowl, so against every instinct he had to take out after the little pip squeak strutting around his yard and teach him a lesson he'd never forget, he sat down.

Roscoe gave a low whistle, signaling Skipper to come back.
It was time to go to plan B.
The only problem was, he didn't have a plan B.
Yet.

"Ah, Roscoe, I don't want to put any pressure on you but Penny Sue has been on the feeder now for over twenty minutes and it's obvious she's getting weaker by each click of the clock." Edgar leaned in close and whispered, "You're running out of time."

"We've got to get Sweetheart away from the window. I think the dog will chase after Skipper if she's not there." Roscoe's mind was racing. He could picture what would happened to Penny Sue if she fell from the feeder. He shuddered and knew he had to think of some way to save her. He didn't have enough time to call in his usual team of Rudy D or the Edelman Brothers. It would take too long for Manny to get in position to go one on one with the dog and judging from its size he doubted if Manny could hold his own if it came down to a real fight.

A thought hit him. "Is Desmond around?"

He heard the word, Desmond, make it's way back through the crowd and someone left the group in search of Desmond.

"It's no use Roscoe, she can't be saved." The thought behind the statement shook him. He turned around and said, "Edgar we can't give up while there's the slightest chance." But, it wasn't Edgar he was facing, it was Desmond.

"Gotcha on that one didn't I?" Desmond prided himself in being able to imitate sounds. He could do voices with uncanny ability. "Let me hear a voice once and it's mine for life," he often said. He drove his teachers in seed school crazy, once answering roll call for every member in class. He did it so well the teacher filled out the attendance sheet having accounted for all of her students. When she looked up, only one of them was seated in front of her and it was Desmond.

"Desmond this is not the time to be…"

"This may not be the best time to bring it up Roscoe but it's Des Mond now. I think it has more of a show business sound to it. Don't you?"

"Desmo… I mean Des Mond we're in a jam. Penny Sue is on the feeder and losing strength by the second. There's a dog at the base of the feeder just waiting for her to fall and we need some way to get Sweetheart away from the window." Roscoe paused to catch his breath.

"Okay. I've got it. Do you have a script of some kind or are we doing improv here?" Des Mond nodded his head from side to side, loosening up, visualizing the scene.

"Improv?" Roscoe asked.

"Improvisation. Making it up as we go along." Des Mond was getting into the problem. "So what are you looking for, the sound of screech owl? A dog barking in the next yard? A car pulling into the driveway? Fireworks? A cat?"

"A door bell," Roscoe answered quickly.

"A door bell?" Des Mond paused, a worried look worked its way across his face. "Gee, that'll take some time Roscoe. You don't just do a doorbell right off the bat. I need to visualize the door and a person stepping on to the porch…"

"There's no time for any of that Des Mond. Now here's what I have in mind." He huddled with Skipper and Des Mond, explaining the plan he'd just improvised.

"So as soon as Sweetheart steps away from the window I take off for the feeder?" Skipper wanted to make sure he had his part right.

"And be careful Skipper, we don't want to loose one squirrel just to save another."

Skipper nodded he understood and moved to his spot by the rose bush at the back of the yard.

Roscoe saw the worried look on Des Mond's face. "I've only heard the doorbell once Roscoe, that was a couple of summers ago and I was pretty young. He held his paws in the air, threw his head back in a dramatic way. "I don't know if I'm up for the part. I was so small and it was in the background." He brought a paw to his forehead and stared hopelessly at the ground.

Roscoe put his paws on his shoulders. "Des Mond. Be the bell."

Des Mond nodded and took off for the front of the house.

Roscoe worked his way around the yard and took his place under a bush near the side of Seed Man's house, ten feet from the feeder.

The dog was concentrating so hard on Penny Sue, struggling to keep her balance, he didn't see the members of the rescue team get into position.

Sweetheart was at the window drinking a cup of tea. She switched her gaze from the top of the feeder to the back of the yard expecting some kind of attack any minute.

Something was going on out there she could feel it.

Roscoe could see her clearly from his place by the side of the house. "Come on Des Mond, show us what you've got," he whispered.

He saw Sweetheart turn her head toward the front of the house, then look back at the feeder. She hesitated for a moment then looked away again. It was obvious she was trying to decide if she should leave her position by the window and see who was at the front door or stay where she was and keep the dog in line.

She set the cup on the table behind her and disappeared from view, curiosity about who would be coming to see her at this time of day won out.

The Squirrel Chronicles: Book One

Roscoe looked to the back of the yard in time to see Skipper leave the tall grass and head for the feeder, looking like he didn't have a care in the world.

He saw the dog shift his attention from the top of the feeder to the back of the yard. His tale flipped from side to side and he made a low, whining noise. He glanced at the window and saw Sweetheart was gone. He stood up to face the intruder.

He took it as long as he could, gave one loud woof and shot away from the base of the feeder in pursuit of Skipper.

The moment he did, Roscoe left the side of the house and scaled the feeder pole. He took Penny Sue's trembling paw and told her everything was going to be okay. Before they headed for the ground he looked out and saw Skipper looping and dipping, sending the dog into long skids as he tried to keep up with his speedy prey.

He saw Sweetheart, puzzled by the doorbell ringing and finding no one there, return to the window. She sized up what was going on and tapped on the window with her knuckle. It was a wasted effort, the dog was totally focused on catching Skipper, regardless of the consequences. To stop now would go against every instinct locked deep in his brain.

Skipper was laughing and taunting as the dog slowed down, gasping, trying to catch his breath. He zipped around in back of the dog who was stretched out on the ground his huge chest heaving. Skipper lifted the dog's tail in victory and all the Community members cheered.

When Roscoe and Penny Sue ducked under the cover of the bush he stopped to give her a chance to rest. The muscles in her arms and legs were still trembling with fatigue.

Finally she looked up at him and he felt lightheaded, he'd never seen anyone more beautiful.

To his surprise Penny Sue leaned forward and gave him a kiss on the cheek. She whispered, "You saved my life and I don't even know your name." Her voice is like an angel's," Roscoe thought. "No," he corrected himself, "more like a choir of angels."

He couldn't take his eyes off of her.

"Your name?" She spoke again and finally Roscoe realized she was talking to him.

"Yes, no question, definitely," he stammered and blushed at having been caught daydreaming. "What was the question?" He asked.

"Guys better get a move on, Bruno's getting his second wind." Skipper dashed over to them and delivered his message then went back to distract the dog in case he decided to try his luck on a couple of slower squirrels.

"Don't even think about it big boy," Roscoe heard Skipper say. The dog rolled over and whined in submission, unable to take another step.

Sweetheart continued tapping on the window, hoping to prod the ferocious beast back into action. When she saw he was down for the count she turned away from the window in disgust.

Roscoe knew it wasn't to answer the doorbell because he'd seen Des Mond run across the yard and join the others in the tall grass.

"We'd better move out Penny Sue, we may not have much time." Roscoe urged, although a quick glance at the condition of the dog would have told him there was no need to hurry. They could have walked across the middle of the yard and stopped in front of him, he was too tired to react.

She took his paw and followed him along the edge of the yard until they reached the others.

Edgar pushed Roscoe aside and embraced Penny Sue.

Roscoe watched them walk towards Edgar's tree. Penny Sue looked back once and whispered a breathless, "Thank you," then blew him a kiss.

He stood for a moment after they disappeared from view. "Thank you is enough," he told himself but even as he said it he knew it wasn't true. He wanted to spend more time with her but under different conditions.

Skipper jogged up beside him. "Hey, I appreciate the work out Roscoe but next time, pick a faster dog. Okay? I mean in less than a minute he was wasted."

"I'll see what I can do Skipper. You did a great job."

"Just a warm up my friend. I'm headed out to do a little road work. You want to come along?" No one could tell by looking at him that he had just spent several minutes staying a step ahead of a vicious dog.

"I'll take a rain check on that." Roscoe felt the worst decision he could make right now would be to try to keep up with Skipper on a run through the Neighborhood.

He headed back to his tree and stretched out with his stomach resting on the floor of his nest and his chin balanced on the top of it. A lot had gone on in a short period of time. He was about to doze off when he heard a voice say, "There's my little hero."

Roscoe rolled over. It was too much to hope that Penny Sue had left Edgar and come to his nest.

He tried to act humble. "Penny Sue any squirrel in the Community would have done… Des Mond, would you stop with the voices?" Des Mond was on a branch close to the nest. "Got you again," he said, "man you're easy."

"No Des Mond, you're good. You sounded just like her. Sorry about making you do the doorbell, I know you're capable of better things." Roscoe envied his ability to impersonate voices and sounds.

"Hey, I should be thanking you. I see a whole new field opening up for me; the sound of doorbells, phones ringing, air conditioners kicking on and off. You've helped broaden my range Roscoe. You caused me to stretch, pushed me out of my comfort zone." Des Mond made big, broad gestures with his arms. "When my agent gets the word out, talent scouts are going to be beating a path to my nest."

"I'll be the first in line for opening night. You were great." Roscoe meant every word of it.

Des Mond left whistling, *If I were a bell I'd be ringing,* and Roscoe rolled back over in his nest.

He replayed all that had happened from the early morning visit by Edgar to seeing Penny Sue for the first time, balanced on the top of the feeder.

"Is that you're name? Roscoe?" Another voice tugged at him from the edge of sleep.

"Des Mond, enough is eno… Penny Sue?" Roscoe sat up and brushed a piece of straw from his fur. Penny Sue was sitting on the branch Des Mond had occupied moments earlier. "What are you doing…? I mean, how did you find…"

"Grandpa Edgar told me all about you." She took a step closer.

"No kidding? He told me about you? I mean, you about me? Edgar I mean?" He wondered why he had so much trouble talking when she was around.

She touched his lips with her paw, suggesting there was no reason to say another word. He reached up and took her paw in his and to his surprise she didn't resist. They left the nest and walked through a green field, under a clear blue sky, toward a ten-pound bag of seeds tucked between two flowering shrubs.

CHAPTER 7

The Eye of the Beholder

Roscoe had fiddled away most of the morning waiting for his turn at the feeder. He was not what most in the Community call a morning squirrel, he liked to sleep in. It wasn't because he stayed up late running around the Neighborhood, it was just his nature to wake up slowly and think about the day ahead of him.

Consequently, by the time he finally got up and did some much needed picking up around his nest, there was a line at the feeder. Usually, by the time he made it up the support rod that held the feeder tubes the good seeds would be gone with only hulls and scraps remaining.

That was the case today. He had to work hard just to get enough to last until his evening meal. He was so engrossed in picking the remaining seeds out of the corner of the feeder tube he didn't notice the bump at the bottom of the support rod.

He totally missed the wobble of the feeder and it wasn't until he felt himself being pushed to one side he became aware something was wrong. He scrambled to get a paw hold someplace but slipped off the feeder and fell to the ground. The last thing he saw before spinning around and landing clumsily was Milton, a normal squirrel in every way except for his terrible eyesight, taking the place he'd just occupied.

Milton had been that way as long as Roscoe could remember. Usually he traveled with a group of friends who would tell him to watch out for the rose bush or be careful because there was a stick in the way.

The friends that looked after him must have been busy because Milton had climbed the support rod on his own and without realizing it, pushed Roscoe off.

"Milton, what do you think you're doing?" There were a few things that really upset Roscoe and someone crowding in line ahead of him was one of them.

Milton looked up and scanned the surroundings. He didn't see anything so he turned to the small opening in the feeder tube.

"Milton, it's me, Roscoe."

Milton looked up again and studied a place on a distant tree where two large branches tied into the trunk.

"Oh, hey Roscoe, I didn't see you there. I'll be through in a minute." He started to dip his head toward the feeder.

"I'm down here Milton. On the ground, below the feeder." This was ridiculous as far as Roscoe was concerned, the guy was a danger to himself and to others. He couldn't believe he'd bumped him off the feeder without knowing it.

"What?" Roscoe could see Milton blink and squint trying to bring things into focus. "Oh, sure, there you are. I was just telling your friend over there," he nodded to the tree trunk, "I'll be finished in a minute."

Roscoe started to say something about didn't he know he'd

pushed him off the feeder but changed his mind. Save your breath, he told himself, it's not worth the effort.

He walked away from the feeder, still hungry, and figured he'd have to wait until evening, he was sure Milton would polish off the few remaining seeds. It was too frustrating talking to someone who kept looking around trying to find out where you were.

He started back to his nest thinking he might have a seed or two tucked away someplace for a situation just like this when he heard a thud.

He turned around and saw Milton on the ground, shaking his head. Roscoe heard him say, "I thought there was a support pole around here someplace."

It looked like he was okay so Roscoe started back across the yard when, out of the corner of his eye, he saw Milton walking straight toward Seed Man's house. He dashed back to the feeder and put his paws on his shoulders, gently turning him around and pointing him toward the back of the yard.

"Is that you Roscoe?" Milton looked at him and blinked. "Thank goodness I caught you in time. I don't think your going to be able to get any seeds this morning because someone removed the support rod. I took a pretty hard fall." He rubbed his shoulder.

"Hey, thanks for the warning Milton, I probably would have missed it." The sarcasm in Roscoe's voice was wasted on Milton.

He watched Milton limp across the yard and waved to the group in the tall grass who'd been looking for him. They gave Roscoe a "We'll take it from here," signal and walked out to meet him.

Roscoe took off towards the path that leads to his tree and nest. He couldn't imagine what it would be like to not to be able to see things clearly. He closed his eyes as he walked and was surprised when he opened them how far he's veered off the path, he would have sworn he was walking in a straight line.

The next morning he felt someone tugging on his foot. He opened one eye slowly and saw his friend Marvin standing at the edge of his nest.

"Ah, Roscoe, sorry to wake you up, but, ah, we've got ourselves a problem."

"Marvin, what are you trying to…" Roscoe doesn't wake up well. He's normally a pleasant, easy going squirrel unless something or someone interrupts his sleep.

"Good, your awake." Marvin didn't seem to pick up the fact the Roscoe was upset. He kept looking toward the ground then back at Roscoe. "Could you step on it Roscoe, I don't think we have a lot of time."

"I've got all the time in the world Marvin. In fact after you leave I'm going to roll over and get a few more minutes sleep. That's how much time I've got."

"I don't think that would be a good idea Rosc, it looks like you've got maybe five seconds." After he said it, Marvin disappeared from the side of the nest.

Roscoe started to pull the small blanket over his shoulders when Marvin's head popped back over the edge of the nest and said, "It's Milton."

They were both on the ground and Marvin pointed to Seed Man's yard as they ran.

Milton was holding on to the feeder pole with both paws. Closer to the house, a roar could be heard coming from a metal box someone had put close to the deck and aimed at the feeder. It created such a vacuum Milton was hanging straight out from the support pole like a flag. His feet were aimed at the metal box and from the look of terror on his face he knew he wasn't going to be able to hold on much longer.

Roscoe quickly sized up the situation. He ran as fast as he could across the yard, left his feet and sailed toward Milton. He grabbed him around the chest and knocked him from the pole. His momentum drove them both out of the range of the pull of the metal box and they rolled safely onto the grass.

They lay still for a moment and Roscoe wondered what would have happened to Milton if he'd taken a second longer to get there.

Milton stood and stretched out a paw to help Roscoe up. "If that's your idea of fun Roscoe, leave me out next time. Okay? It's not a good idea to try to crowd ahead of someone in the seed line." He turned around trying to figure out where he was.

Roscoe couldn't believe it. He'd risked his life for him and now he thought it was because he was trying to cut in front of him to get to the feeder. "Milton you were about to be…" He stopped and watched a bird flutter from a tree branch over to the feeder. It was about to land on the feeder perch when it came into the range of the vacuum. There was a brief, "Chirp," and it was gone, sucked into the metal box with only one brown feather remaining behind. Roscoe watched it float to the ground.

"That could have been you Milton." Roscoe was on his feet pointing to the metal box, his voice shaking with emotion. "You could have joined that bird in the metal box if I hadn't saved you."

"What bird? What box?" Milton asked as he looked around and blinked.

Two of Milton's friends came up and put their arms around his shoulder. They turned him away from the house and started toward the back of the yard.

"Thanks Roscoe," one of them hollered over his shoulder. "We looked away for a minute and the next thing we knew we saw him hanging on to the feeder pole. We didn't know what to do so we asked Marvin to get you, we were sure you'd think of something."

They were half way across the yard and the one doing the talking knew it was hard for Roscoe to hear over the roar of the fan in the box so he waved.

Roscoe heard the noise from the metal box diminish and gradually turn to a low hum. He looked at the box then moved his gaze to the big picture window at the back of Seed Man's house.

He could see two humans standing there watching what had gone on in the yard. One wore a tan uniform and a ball cap. On the front of the cap was a badly drawn picture of a squirrel with a red X stitched over it. He noticed some words printed above the squirrel's head. He looked closer and saw, in bright red letters, *"SQUIRREL AWAY"* and below the image of the squirrel, *"Your One Stop Anti-squirrel Store."*

He didn't recognize the person next to the man in the uniform at first but knew it wasn't Seed Man. Then he realized he was mistaken, it wasn't a he it was Sweetheart. Her hair was in curlers and she wore a pink, quilted housecoat with a feathery collar. She was pointing at the metal box and asking the man in the uniform questions about it.

Roscoe finally put two and two together; the humans at the window and the box on the ground. Then he heard the low, grinding sound of small gears starting to mesh. He glanced at the metal box and watched as it slowly turned until the opening was facing him.

From somewhere deep in the box a fan clicked on and he

could feel the first gentle tug of air on his fur as the motor began to pick up speed.

He was so fascinated by the movement of the box and the sound of gears turning he was unaware of the force that started to gently pull him forward, he almost waited too long to leave.

It took all his strength to jump to one side and escape the vacuums grasp. He took one last look at the box and saw the same squirrel with the red X drawn over it that was on the uniformed man's cap. He saw the words, "SQUIRREL AWAY," written on the side of the box. Beneath it was a bright red arrow pointing away from the front of the box and Roscoe figured it indicated the direction of air flow. *"Out of sight Out of mind,"* was printed beneath the arrow.

The box began to turn toward his new location, its movement controlled by the human in the tan uniform. The last thing Roscoe noticed before he took off across the yard was Sweetheart standing at the window laughing and clapping her hands.

"So what do you think we should do Roscoe?" Edgar, Chairman of the Committee for the Protection of Neighborhood Resources asked. He'd called an evening meeting of the Committee and invited anyone in the Community interested in coming up with some way to deal with the menacing *Squirrel Away* problem to join them.

It was no longer a matter of Milton's safety, it posed a problem for anyone going to the feeder.

Roscoe wasn't a member of the Committee but he'd been asked to tell everyone about his experience with the menace since he was the only one who'd actually seen it in action.

The meeting was supposed to take place in the Committee meeting room in the base of Edgar's tree but so many had shown up it was obvious there wasn't going to be enough room. So, Edgar had moved the meeting to the Clearing in front of his tree.

He'd had sent one of the younger squirrels to see if the metal box was still there. He'd returned with the report that it was and only the human in the tan uniform was still at the window. It had taken awhile for him to get back because he couldn't resist watching the box swing slowly from one side of the yard to the other looking for unsuspecting prey. He was finally pulled away when Edgar sent a second runner to see what was taking so long.

"Well for one thing, I know I'm going to need Sparky on this one." Sparky is the only member of the Community who is skilled in figuring out technical things. Because of his unusual appearance and strange habits he had been made fun of through his three years at seed school. But, that all changed when he was able to come up with away to open the automatic garage doors so Roscoe and his team could recover the feeder post and tubes a few weeks earlier.

He looked the part of a technical genius. The hair on his head was fuzzy and stuck out in all directions. His body fur was matted down in places and dull brown showing he'd spent more time in his laboratory than outside in the sun getting exercise. He was always working on a problem of some kind and refused to "hang out" with other squirrels his age. When someone asked why he'd told them he had better things to do than waste time sitting around talking about unimportant things and some in the Community took it the wrong way. But Roscoe had come to his defense and explained that as far as Sparky was concerned, if they weren't talking about science he didn't have a lot to say.

Of course the now famous removal of the feeder from the

garage had caused members of the Community to see him in a new way.

Sparky stepped through the crowd and walked over to Roscoe. "I was studying the box earlier and I've got a couple of ideas." Roscoe smiled, he wasn't surprised that Sparky was already way ahead of him.

"I'm going to need Manny and six of the strongest members in the Community." Roscoe added.

His request to have Manny on his team surprised some who were gathered there. Manny had always been big for his age but lately he'd ballooned to where he could barely leave his nest to eat. He forced members of the community to bring him seeds from the feeder by threatening to visit their nest in the middle of the night and pay them back. They knew he and Roscoe had worked together in the past and their only fear was they would be the one sent to talk him into being part of the operation. He was not the most pleasant squirrel normally and they hated to think what he would be like if they were the one to have to wake him up.

"They're yours Roscoe. We'll figure out who the six strongest are and send them over first thing in the morning." Edgar leaned toward Roscoe and said, "I take it from your requests you have a plan." He smiled, proud that he'd been the one to bring him in to work on the problem.

"Not really sir," Roscoe had to be honest about it. When he saw the surprised look on Edgar's face he quickly added, "But thanks to you I have a team of clever people and I'm sure we can come up with something. Let's meet in the morning to finalize our plans."

He started to leave when a thought hit him. "Has anyone seen E. Paul lately?"

If all you had to go on was the response from the Committee members you would have thought Roscoe had said a bad word when he mentioned E. Paul's name. Most on the Committee stepped back and took a sudden interest in the trees around them.

Edgar bit his lip and looked at the ground.

From the day he was old enough to go out of the nest alone E. Paul had been different. While others jumped and played he could be found crouched down, looking at a marigold or staring at his reflection in a pool of water. As he grew older he spent less time with kids his own age and more by himself. He had a natural gift for drawing and instead of attending seed school like the other squirrels, he'd take his pad and a few stubs of charcoal to the edge of Seed Man's yard looking for something interesting to draw.

You were never sure when he would show up. You might wake up in the morning and find him perched on the edge of your nest sketching you. He would then offer it for sale under the title, *Squirrel Waking*.

He wore the fur around his head pulled together and formed into a series of long spikes.

He'd let the light fur under his chin grow longer than was considered acceptable by most in the Community.

He was Edgar's oldest son.

"I'm sure you mean no harm by your question Roscoe." Edgar had recovered from the blow delivered at the mention of his name. "To be honest with you we, that is the Edna and I, are never sure exactly where he is."

He hated to have to mention it out loud because he was the Committee member in charge of the, *"Do you know where your child is tonight?"* program at seed school.

"Well, if you see him, tell him I'd like to talk to him. I have a little project that would be right down his alley." Roscoe spoke quietly; he didn't think the others needed to hear.

Like most parents of wayward children, Edgar grabbed at any chance to help others see his son in a different light.

The meeting broke up and Roscoe and Sparky walked toward Roscoe's nest. Sparky waved his paws around explaining something about switches and connectors. The information sailed right over Roscoe's head. But as he'd told Sparky before, "It's not important that I understand it. The important thing is that you do."

Edgar led a dozen husky young squirrels over to a part of the yard where there were some large stones. He planned to have them lift and carry the stones around until only the six strongest remained standing.

Roscoe felt there was no need to get Manny yet; he wouldn't be needed until he got some kind of plan together.

When Roscoe reached the ground early the next morning he was met at the base of his tree by six muscular squirrels. They each had a large stone in their paws. A couple of them were doing pushups. They wore small checkered bandannas tied around their head and all but one had on tight leather gloves.

If it weren't for the Community problem they now faced Roscoe would have had nothing to do with any of this group. They were loud and rough and if there was any trouble in the Community like fights or arguments, it was usually caused by the members of this group.

"Edgar said we was to come over this morning and meet up with you here Rosc." Roscoe recognized Dirk, the spokesman for the group. "He, Edgar I mean, said we was to come over and do whatever you told us to." When he finished talking the rest of the group gathered around Roscoe anxious to find out their part in defeating the backyard menace.

"Has anyone seen Sparky?" Roscoe managed to squeak out. He was having trouble looking past Dirk and his boys. They were at least a head taller then him and twice as big in the arms and chest. When they stood shoulder to shoulder they formed a solid wall around him.

"Skinny kid? Funny looking fur?" Dirk asked.

"Yes, that sounds about right." Roscoe was afraid to say more.

"Lou. Chester. Get the goofy looking kid down from the tree and bring him over here." Dirk made a motion with his head and two from the group took off for a nearby tree.

In the open space created when the two left, Roscoe could see Sparky hanging from a branch, his feet barely touching the ground. Someone, Roscoe figured it was Dirk or one of his boys, had hooked the back of his lab coat over a broken tree limb as a practical joke. He could see the plastic pocket protector Sparky always wore in his lab coat pocket lying on the ground.

Lou and Chester lifted Sparky off the branch and set his feet on the ground. "Sorry kid," Roscoe heard one of them say, "we didn't know. You know?" The other one picked up his pocket protector and handed it to him.

They led Sparky over to Roscoe and took their place in the circle again.

"You okay Sparky?" Roscoe was concerned. Sparky looked a little pale and somewhat shaken from his experience. Right now Roscoe needed a clear thinking Sparky not one still wondering what mischief the six stone carriers were going to do to him next.

"Oh, yea, sure, definitely. Ah, actually, I had an idea while I was up there," he nodded with his head toward the branch on the tree. "I was only up there an hour or so, I slept through most of it."

"Okay then, Dirk, have one of your team get Manny. When he shows up operation, *Away With Squirrel's Away*, can get started." Roscoe rubbed his paws together, anxious to get going.

"I don't think that's such a good idea there Roscoe." Dirk had a funny look on his face and stepped back an inch or two.

"What's the problem, you haven't even heard my plan to…"

"The, get Manny part of your plan is what I'm talking about," Dirk interrupted Roscoe. "It might be best to send someone other than one of us." The five other squirrels nodded in agreement.

Roscoe got a funny sound in his voice and said, "What's a matter, de big bad squirrels afraid of widdle Manny?" After he said it he realized from the looks on their faces he wasn't far from the truth.

"Yea, something like that. It goes back a long way, we don't need to go into it now." Dirk was looking at the ground as he spoke, making little circles in the dirt with his foot.

"I'll get him," Sparky spoke up and squeezed between the group surrounding he and Roscoe.

"I guess we'll have to wait until Sparky gets back but we're loosing valuable time." Roscoe was upset, he expected more cooperation from them.

"Ah, Roscoe, if you would just tell us what were supposed to do then we could, like, not be around when Manny shows up." Dirk kept looking over his shoulder as he spoke.

"Good grief," was all Roscoe could think of to say. He crouched down and drew his plan in the dirt. He sketched the edge of Seed Man's yard and his house. When he asked if they were able to follow him this far they nodded yes. He drew the feeder and then the *Squirrel's Away* vacuum hood between the feeder and the edge of the deck. Roscoe looked up and they nodded again. He drew a circle around the *Squirrel's Away* box and a line from it to a new place on ground. He drew a larger version of the metal box and described how it worked. Sparky had gone over the same material with him the night before.

He told the Stone Team what they were supposed to do and where they were supposed to go. They nodded they understood. Each member put a paw in the center of the circle and lifted them up while saying, "Stone team," in their deep voices. They each picked up the stone they'd carried over and left to take their place by the rose bush at the side of the yard.

About the time the last member of the Stone Team was out of sight Manny and Sparky showed up.

"Let's go over to the command post," Roscoe told them, "nothing can happened until the guy in the uniform gets here."

"Uniform Man," Sparky corrected him. "I've been calling him Uniform Man. It's simpler than saying the human in the tan uniform."

Roscoe smiled as they walked to the command post, calling him Uniform Man worked for him. He stopped when he saw E. Paul leaning with his back against a tree.

"Like, I heard you needed me for a gig of some kind. True?" While E. Paul spoke Roscoe checked him out. It had been awhile since he'd seen him. He was taller than he remembered but that may have been more of an illusion created by the long black coat he was wearing.

"Oh, hey, E. Paul I was afraid you wouldn't be able to make it." Roscoe motioned for the others to continue on while he dropped back and talked to E. Paul. He told him the job he had in mind was the final step in dealing with the metal box.

"That's not the way I work man," E. Paul was shaking his head and stepping back. "I mean what's my motivation? What kind of statement am I trying to make? What is there about this work that would move or inspire me to become involved?" He looked at Roscoe, "I don't see any passion here, do you see what I'm saying?"

Roscoe explained the Community was in danger. No one could go to the feeder with out being pulled into the metal box and as a result they would either starve or have to move. There was the additional risk that someone might become desperate enough to go to the feeder and be pulled into the metal box.

"So, this is like, a small group of squirrels fighting against the big machine thing. Am I right?" E Paul was looking across the yard at the metal box.

Roscoe nodded yes.

"And tell me again, like, what did it say on the side of the box?" E. Paul pulled a small notepad from a pocket in his long black coat and started writing.

He left with the promise that if thought of anything he'd show up but he gave no guarantee. "You can't force art Roscoe," he'd explained in a serious tone, "it just has to happen."

Roscoe caught up with Sparky and asked if he'd been able to figure out what to do with the metal box. Sparky yawned and told him it had taken a while but sure, it was taken care of. Sparky was the last person to say he'd been up all night doing some very complicated rewiring work. He loved the challenge of solving difficult problems and that was the only reward he needed.

Roscoe, Sparky and Manny took their place at the command center under the tree limb at the back of the yard.

Marvin and Jules saw what was going on and came over and

asked if they could join them. They had Milton with them and all three pushed in under the tree branch.

"Surveillance is what were doing Milton, in case you're wondering," Marvin whispered. He was pleased he'd remembered the word Roscoe had taught him and was anxious to use it and impress his friend. "It means waiting and watching."

"Oh, right," Milton answered while he looked around to locate Marvin. He ended up facing away from the house.

Sparky tapped Roscoe on the shoulder. "Is that our guy?" He was pointing at a man in the tan uniform wearing a ball cap, standing at the picture window.

"That's him. That's Uniform Man." Roscoe felt the rush of excitement that always came before an operation got underway. Once things got started he was steady as a rock but it was probably because so many things could go wrong even with the most thought out plan he was feeling a little nervous.

He gave a low whistle and waved his arm, directing the Stone Team to get in position.

At the same time, he tapped Manny on his massive shoulder and whispered, "Show time." Manny nodded okay and started across the yard in his usual slow, rolling motion.

Roscoe glanced at the picture window in time to see a surprised look come across Uniform Man's face when he saw Manny coming towards him. He held up the remote control and pushed a button that started swinging the metal box around so the opening was facing Manny.

He pushed another button and waited for the vacuum motors to kick on.

Nothing happened.

Roscoe could see confusion sweep across the man's face. This was his equipment and its makers guaranteed it would work under any condition.

Manny leaned against the feeder support post happy for the chance to rest.

Uniform Man pushed the button on the gray box again and he got the same result as the first time. He disappeared from the window and Roscoe motioned for the Stone Team to move out.

They slipped in from the side of the yard and set the stones they were carrying on the ground near the metal box. One of them started removing the screws around the base of the box while the others anxiously waited.

With that task out of the way they lifted the top of the box off and set it on the ground near them.

As soon as the top was removed a bird flew out and headed for a branch on a tree at the back of the yard. The bird was followed by a small dog that looked bewildered by what had happened; spending a night in a metal box with a chirping bird was a far cry from sleeping in a warm bed in his owners bedroom. He whined a few times and sat down not sure what to do, the whole *Squirrel Away* experience had left him bewildered.

They checked to make sure the metal box was empty then Stone Team picked up the stones they'd brought with them and put them in the metal box like Roscoe had told them. When they finished they lifted the lid up and put it back on, finally replacing and tightening the screws that held it down.

They looked to the command post and raised their muscular arms in victory.

Roscoe motioned for them to get away quickly, they could do their celebrating later.

As the last one was disappearing into the tall grass Uniform Man slid the back door open and stepped onto the deck. "I bet he thinks the glass in the window is interfering with his remote control," Sparky muttered.

Roscoe had no idea what he was talking about.

Uniform Man pushed on the little lever that caused the box to turn. He was relieved when he saw it start to move. He watched it swing slowly around and end up facing him. He was so pleased to see the metal box responding to his command he missed the significance of its position.

He pushed on the button that started the motor and relaxed when he heard the first sound of gears turning and the motor picking up speed. His first sense that something was wrong came when instead of feeling a tug of air from the metal box he felt a push. While he was trying to figure out what could have gone wrong in the motor wiring the first stone flew out of the metal box and smacked against the deck rail next to him.

He watched in amazement as the box turned slightly, adjusting its aim, and sent a second stone sailing over his head, coming close enough to clip the bill on his baseball cap and sending it skidding across the deck.

Uniform Man realized something had gone terribly wrong with his equipment and turned to go back in the house. He opened the door to the kitchen and closed it just before a third stone banged against the door frame.

It wasn't long before Roscoe saw the top of his head peek over the bottom of the picture window. He stood slowly and pushed madly on the buttons of the remote control.

The metal box turned again, stopping so it was pointing at the window. Uniform Man shook his head in disbelief. Another figure joined him, Roscoe was sure it was Sweetheart. She seemed to be asking what was wrong about the time he grabbed her and they both disappeared from view.

A fourth stone was launched and took out the picture window in one shattering blow. A fifth and sixth sailed through the empty space where the window used to be and Roscoe heard glass break somewhere inside but had know idea what had been hit.

Smoke started coming out of the box and Roscoe heard the screech of gears grinding and the vacuum motor winding down.

For a moment it was quiet then a cheer erupted from the stone team.

Roscoe looked towards the deck in time to see E. Paul step out and walk slowly to the metal box. He had a paw under his chin and stroked the few long hairs that formed his beard. He paced back and forth, deep in thought, stopping occasionally to rub the top of his head and then start walking again.

Finally he dropped his paw, smiled and went to work.

Things remained quiet in the back yard. Once Roscoe had seen Sweetheart and Uniform Man peek over the sill of what once had been the picture window and then quickly duck away. Marvin ran over and said he'd heard Uniform Man's truck pull out of the driveway and go up the street.

Finally Roscoe thought it was safe so he left the command post and walked across the yard to the metal box to see what E. Paul had come up with.

He had been so skillful in painting over some things and adding other things it was hard to remember what the original message on the side of the box was.

He smiled when he saw what he'd done. Instead of, *"Squirrel Away,"* it said, *"Squirel's Always Win,"* in big red letters. Next to it was the picture of a squirrel with its paws in the air standing on top of a big red X. Under the arrow that was now painted dark blue was written, *"They'll drive you out of your mind."*

The familiar, eP, E. Paul's signature, was printed below the lettering.

The rest of the Community joined him at the metal box and stood quietly next to the burned out box. It isn't everyday your able to shut down a threat to the Community and make a statement while doing it.

Marvin was the first to speak up. "Last one to the feeder is a house cat."

Roscoe waited a moment before joining them; he wanted to enjoy this brief moment of victory. Before going up the feeder support post he glanced at the back of the yard. He saw Edgar with one arm around E. Paul's shoulder make a big, sweeping motion with his other arm, a gesture. Roscoe figured he was describing a picture that someday would hang behind his desk in the Committee meeting room if E Paul could find the proper motivation.

Occasionally squirrels do win, Roscoe told himself and said he needed to remember that.

He thought it was a shame Milton had missed the excitement. He'd been facing the wrong the whole time.

CHAPTER 8

The Attack of the Mutant Squirrels

"Hey, Roscoe, who's the new guy?" Marvin tapped Roscoe on the shoulder and pointed to the squirrel hopping in a large circle around the backyard of Seed Man's house.

Roscoe shrugged. "He's not from around here, I'm sure of that." He turned and continued digging up a nut he'd buried last fall but something was bothering him about the stranger in the yard. He stopped what he was **doing** and took a closer look. He was puzzled by the odd, jerky movements of the newcomer as he made his way around the yard.

It finally dawned on him what it was, he was perfect. Every jump was exactly the same. Everything from the color of his fur to the sparkle in his eye was flawless.

In fact, he decided that was the problem, he was too perfect.

"I'm going to see what I can find out about him," Marvin hollered. He'd been sitting on his back legs, watching the new guy circle the yard. He dropped on all four's and headed to a spot that would put him directly in the path of the advancing squirrel.

"Marvin hold on a second, something's wrong." About the time Roscoe finished saying it he saw something move at the side of the deck. It wasn't much, just enough to make him curious. He studied the area closely and it looked like someone was on their hands and knees, creeping forward, trying to get a better look at what was going on in the yard.

He could see the top of a brown baseball cap as the human edged closer to the corner of the deck. He recognized the familiar logo of *Squirrel Away*; a squirrel with a big red X stitched over it. He knew instantly the person wearing the cap was the one the Community called Uniform Man.

He gave a quick glance at the big picture window at the back of Seed Man's house and saw Sweetheart looking out, watching what was going on.

He noticed Marvin had stopped and sat down, waiting for the stranger to complete the part of the circle that would bring him his way. He had his usual friendly look, open and trusting. The general talk around the Community of Abner was Marvin was a squirrel who never met a stranger.

Roscoe saw Marvin's tail twitch as the newcomer made the final turn and started towards him.

He saw Uniform Man shift his position and aim a gray box at the squirrel.

"Marvin, get out of there, it's a trap," Roscoe screamed at the top of his voice.

Marvin turned and looked his way. He raised his shoulders and put one paw to his ear, telling Roscoe he didn't hear what he said.

Poof, the new squirrel had come within a few feet of Marvin and exploded, sending a plume of gray powder in the air that gently settled over him.

Roscoe saw Marvin blink then watched as he started swaying from side to side. His lips formed an odd smile then he fell to the ground, face first.

Uniform Man broke from the side of the deck and started a slow jog across the yard to retrieve the unconscious Marvin stretched out on the grass, the funny smile still on his face. Uniform Man carried a net in one hand and the gray metal box in the other.

Showing no concern for his own safety, Roscoe took off across the yard towards Marvin. When he got there a sweet smell still hung in the air. He felt dizzy but figured the most powerful part of the powder released by the exploding squirrel had blown away. He grabbed Marvin by the shoulders and dragged him to the edge of the yard.

"You've got to spend less time at the feeder," Roscoe muttered as he strained to pull him past the rose bush and into the tall grass. He found the hollowed out place in the ground he was looking for and they both fell in it. He reached up, pulled some grass over them and waited.

When his breathing was finally back to normal, he stuck his head up high enough to see over the top of the grass. He watched as Uniform Man poked under the rose bush with the handle of the net and was glad he hadn't chosen that as their hiding place.

He saw him straighten and look for other possible hiding places. He was about to head back to the house when Marvin moaned; he was starting to come around.

Uniform Man stopped, pushed his head forward and turned slightly sure he'd heard something.

Roscoe clamped his paw over Marvin's mouth and waited to see if that would be enough to keep Uniform Man from coming their way.

Uniform Man took a step toward them then stopped and listened for the slightest sound that would help him zero in on their location.

Roscoe heard it at the same time Uniform Man did, a moan coming from the other side of the yard.

The first moan was followed by a second, but this time a touch of agony had been added. Uniform Man spun around and looked in the direction of the moan, it was clear from his actions he was confused. He knew he'd seen the two squirrels head towards this part of the yard and was wondering how they could have ended up over there?

The next moan decided it for him, he took off in the direction of the new sound.

"I bet it's Des Mond," Roscoe whispered to Marvin, "that guy can imitate anything."

He poked his head up and watched Uniform Man swing his net through the grass, hoping to find who ever he'd heard that was in such pain. He finally gave up and walked slowly back to the house.

Roscoe watched as he looked at Sweetheart who was still at the window. He shook his head, telling her he couldn't find them. She tapped the window and pointed to the tall grass where the Roscoe and Marvin were hiding.

"We better get a move on," Roscoe whispered to the groggy Marvin.

"Of course. Of course." Marvin had a dreamy quality to his voice. "Moving on. It's moving day Roscoe." He giggled. "Moving day, moving away. What do you say? It's moving day."

The Squirrel Chronicles: Book One

They headed for the nearest tree and Roscoe helped his friend climb up. When he was sure he was okay he ventured out on a limb that gave a clear view of the backyard. He watched Uniform Man lift a backpack off the ground and set it on the deck. He undid the buckles that held the straps in place and flipped the cover open. He reached into the pack and to Roscoe's amazement, pulled out a squirrel that looked exactly like the one he'd seen explode.

He adjusted something on the back of the impostor squirrel, closed up the pack, laced the straps back through the buckles and set the squirrel on the ground at the corner of the deck. He crouched down, gave it a push, and scooted back, out of sight.

Roscoe gave a quick glance at the window. He saw Sweetheart with her hands on her hips. The look on her face said, "It had better work this time or I'm calling another pest control service." She was anxious to get rid of the squirrels before Seed Man got back from his business trip. She could imagine their conversation when he returned.

Seed Man: "Where are the squirrels, I haven't seen one at the feeder all day?"

Her: "Oh? No squirrels? I really hadn't noticed."

From his position in the tree, looking down on the backyard, Roscoe wondered how anyone could have thought the impostor, following the same path as the first one, was real. For one thing, neither one stopped at the feeder for seeds; that alone should have been a tip off. For another, it just kept going around the yard in a big circle, never looking around to make sure it was safe and never stopping to search for buried nuts.

He decided It was time to get some help. He was afraid to leave Marvin in the tree so he helped him down, stopped the first Community member he came to and asked if he'd seen

Sparky. Sparky is the Community genius. He has little regard for his appearance and sometimes stands for hours in one place, barely moving as his mind races through possible answers to difficult questions.

"The last time I saw him he was over by the elm tree," the squirrel replied and continued on to another part of the woods.

Roscoe found Sparky standing directly under a tree limb. He was holding a small device with wires that ran to a connection on the helmet he was wearing and was deep in thought.

"Sparky, what's going on?" Roscoe approached him slowly, not wanting to take him by surprise.

Sparky looked up and blinked. The look in his eyes suggested he'd been spending quality time in some far off, scientific world. He waved and said, "Oh, hi Rosc."

His greeting was followed by, "Watch out!" and he pushed Roscoe aside just in time to keep him from getting hit by a walnut that fell from a branch overhead.

Sparky looked up. "Nigel, did I say drop the nut?'

Roscoe heard someone in the tree mumble something he couldn't make out. If it was Nigel, he was lost among the leaves and branches.

"Watch my paw Nigel. Wait until I wave my paw. Remember we talked about that?" Sparky shook his head; he had trouble with anyone that didn't think at the same level he did, which basically meant he had trouble with everyone in the Community.

Roscoe heard something overhead that sounded like, "Okay or Oh hey or Is it time for lunch yet," he wasn't sure.

"Sparky I need to talk to you." Sparky was looking at the box in his hand, Roscoe wasn't sure he'd heard him.

"Right. Right. Hold on a second." He raised his paw in the air and swung it back and forth. He put his arms to his side and looked straight ahead.

Nothing happened. He looked up. "Nigel, drop the nut." Roscoe could tell by the sound of his voice that he was upset.

"Sorry," came from above. A nut fell and made a direct hit on the top of the helmet Sparky was wearing. Sparky waved his paw to say that was good, the experiment was over.

Another nut came hurtling from high in the tree and bounced close to Sparky's foot.

"Enough," he hollered up to Nigel.

"Sorry, but you waved your paw and I..." Nigel hollered back. Roscoe could hear him move across a tree limb and start toward the ground.

"I knew they were wrong," Sparky sounded pleased. "Take a look at this," he turned the box toward Roscoe who saw a screen with numbers across the top and down one side.

Roscoe pushed it back toward Sparky and shrugged his shoulders. "I don't get it."

"Well this number across the top is the force of the nut hitting my helmet. See, I've set up a strain matrix across the top of the helmet. It measures the dynamic load when the nut hits the matrix and subtracts..." He stopped when he saw Roscoe waving his paw.

"Oh, sorry," he blushed when he realized he'd gone too far with his explanation. "The top line tells how hard it hit, the numbers on the side show fast it was going." He made a funny face, he was much more comfortable explaining things in a technical way. "Where the two lines intersect shows the force at im..., ah, that is, how hard it hits the top of the helmet."

"Which proves?" Roscoe was trying to help him along.

"Oh, yea, right." Sometime Sparky got so caught up in

technical details he lost sight of the big picture. "The practice of dropping nuts on the heads of members who break Community rules, is a bad one." He got a serious look on his face and pointed to his head. "Unless you're wearing a helmet it could cause permanent damage."

Roscoe didn't know what to say; nut dropping on rule breakers had been a practice in the Community for as long as he could remember. No one had ever challenged the wisdom of the practice before.

"The farther the nut falls of course, the more damage it causes. Look at this graph." He pulled a clipboard from his briefcase and turned it so Roscoe could see. "I'm presenting this data to Edgar and the Committee to Protect Neighborhood Resources. What better resource is there for the Committee to protect than us? And yet they do something like this."

In all that had gone on, Roscoe almost forgot why he'd come over. "If you've got a minute I'd like you to see something."

"Sure, no problem." Sparky talked while he removed his helmet and handed it and the clipboard to Nigel who'd come out of the tree and was standing next to him. "Will you take this back to the lab, I'll meet you there in a few minutes."

Nigel started to apologize about dropping the last nut but decided not to since Sparky hadn't said anything. He took the items from Sparky and headed for the lab.

The fur around Sparky's head was a mess, keeping the same shape it had been in the helmet but he didn't seem to notice.

"What's up?" He asked as they moved to a place at the back of the yard.

"That." Roscoe pointed to the imitation squirrel completing another lap around the yard.

"Cute," Sparky said. "Looks like a mutant, model M701B.

There's a picture of them in the *Squirrel Away* catalog."

"How'd you get a catalog from *Squirrel Away*?" Roscoe couldn't believe it.

"Well, let's just say I borrowed it from off the deck during our last little run in with Uniform Man. It must have dropped out of his pocket when he was chasing us."

Sparky kicked at a little clod of dirt, embarrassed that he been caught taking something from Seed Man's house without saying anything about it to Roscoe.

"Actually, I didn't take it, Louie did." That seemed to make it all right, he looked up at Roscoe and smiled.

"Light Paws Louie? You know Light Paws?" Roscoe couldn't believe it, he'd only heard of Louie, very few squirrels had ever seen him. "Keep your hand on your wallet whenever Light Paws is around," had been a saying in the Community of Abner for as long as he could remember.

"You wouldn't happened to know where he is now would you?" Roscoe knew it was a long shot but didn't think it would hurt to ask.

"Sure. My place." Sparky said it like it was the most natural thing in the world. "Where else would my brother stay when he comes for a visit?"

"Light Paws is your brother?" Roscoe was dumbfounded.

"Keep it down will you," Sparky put a paw on Roscoe's shoulder," that kind of information is on a need to know basis." He looked Roscoe in the eye until he was sure he understood.

"Your secret's safe with me," Roscoe tried to reassure him, "but I need to talk to him as soon as possible."

After telling Marvin to keep an eye on Uniform Man and to let him know if he anything unusual happens, he and Sparky headed for the lab.

Roscoe waited while Sparky punched in the code to open the lab door, then followed him inside. He had never been in the lab, he'd only heard about it from friends who'd caught a glimpse inside when Sparky was entering or leaving.

Open boxes with wires projecting from them covered the top of the work bench that lined the lab walls. Catalogs of various types were stacked on the floor. A chalk board, covered with notes and calculations was hung between two lockers that held electronic equipment.

"You'll have to wear this," Sparky slipped a loop of plastic over Roscoe's head that had a visitors badge clipped to it. As a way of explanation he said, "It's just a formality, everyone has to wear one."

Sparky started going through one of the stacks of catalogs while Roscoe walked around the lab and examined some of the items on the workbench. That's when he noticed Light Paws leaning against a locker.

"Hey Louie I didn't see you there, ah, how's it going?" It took Roscoe a second to recover from the surprise of seeing him, somehow he'd missed him when he'd looked around the room the first time.

"Think nothing of it man," Louie straightened and walked over to him and touched paws. There was so much Roscoe wanted to ask him. His reputation as a thief had grown to the point that a number of Communities had trading cards with his picture on the front and were exchanged by students at seed school. On the back of the card was a description of things he had taken from humans and carried a notice in bold letters that he never stole from members of the Community.

"We could really use your help today Louie, we've got a major problem." Roscoe couldn't get over the thought that he was actually talking to the famous Light Paws Louie.

"Hey, your problem is my problem, let's get Sparky and talk about it." He turned to go over to his brother but stopped and faced Roscoe. "Here's your visitor's badge." He handed Roscoe the badge still attached to the plastic loop he'd slipped over his head earlier.

"Incredible," Roscoe said as he put the visitors badge back on. He hadn't noticed him taking it, they'd only been talking for a couple of seconds.

They joined Sparky at the stack of catalogs and started thinking about what could be done to end the reign of the mutant squirrels.

They hadn't been working on the problem long when they heard a knock on the lab door. Sparky looked at the monitor over his workbench and saw Marvin pacing back and forth outside, unaware he was being watched.

"It's your buddy Marvin," he told Roscoe as he crossed the lab floor and opened the door. Marvin stepped in and was immediately giving a visitors badge.

"Uniform Man left the yard a few minutes ago Roscoe." Marvin was out of breath from his run to the lab. "I think he'll be gone for awhile; he left in his truck." Then as an after thought he added, "Sweetheart is still at the window though."

"We'd better get a move on then," Roscoe headed for the door. "I'll explain what I have in mind on the way there."

"Don't forget these," Louie was holding up the visitor badges he'd taken from Roscoe and Marvin.

"Incredible," they both said touching their chests where the had last seen their badge.

Roscoe explained to Marvin he was going to have to keep Sweetheart watching from the window while Louie made his way across the side of the yard and over to the backpack under the deck.

"Is there a chance this thing is going to, you know, explode or anything. It was a little spooky last time." Marvin had a worried look on his face.

"You know what to expect now Marvin," Roscoe tried to console him. "I don't think it will catch you off guard this time."

"They have to stop before they explode," Sparky added. "As long as he's moving you've got nothing to worry about. When he stops take off. Besides, we don't know if Sweetheart can make them blow up or not. There may only be one activation device."

Marvin stepped out of the tall grass and took a first hesitant step toward the mutant squirrel.

From their spot at the control center behind the big limb that dips down at the back of the yard, Roscoe and Sparky watched Louie dash across the open space between the edge of the yard and the house. When he got there he pulled the backpack from under the deck and with unbelievable speed, opened it and looked inside. He poked around for a second or two, then held up the little gray box for Sparky to see.

Marvin stopped and watched in amazement as the mutant squirrel hopped past him and continued in the big circle around the yard. He had to resist the urge to trip him.

"That's it," Sparky spoke and gestured for Louie to redo the straps on the pack and join them at the back of the yard. "It looks like there's only one activation device, otherwise Marvin would be a goner." Sparky was mumbling, talking more to himself than to Roscoe. "He can't seem to take his eyes off the decoy."

Louie seemed to appear out of nowhere and joined them at the command post.

"Here you go bro," he handed the gray box to Sparky.

Sparky immediately slipped the sharp edge of a screwdriver in the corner of the of the box and snapped the top off.

Roscoe and Louie watched as Sparky stared at the inside of the box. He mumbled something about it being state of the art and it was going to be a real challenge then grew quiet and studied the wiring in the box.

Roscoe had never seen Sparky at work before, he'd only seen the results of his labor. He knew he preferred to work alone in his lab where he didn't have an audience asking him what he was doing every five minutes. Roscoe would have given anything to be able to see what was going on inside that fantastic mind of his.

Sparky continued to stare at the box, not moving a muscle, the picture of concentration.

Marvin hopped over and joined them. "Ah guys, better get a move on, Uniform Man just pulled up in his truck."

Roscoe motioned for Marvin to stop talking. He knew better than to have anything interrupt Sparky while he was thinking. It wouldn't do any good to try to hurry him, in moments like this he moved at his own pace.

Suddenly Sparky shook his head and smiled.

"He's got it," Louie whispered.

"Got what?" Marvin was trying to figure out what was going on. "What's he got Roscoe?"

Sparky pulled a couple of wires loose and clipped them with small pair of pliers he'd brought with him. He twisted a different pair of wires together and stuck them back in the box.

He snapped the cover back on the box and handed it to Louie. "Sorry it took so long. I hadn't seen anything like that before. See the inverter circuit was hidden beneath the…"

"Save it Sparks, you don't have to explain anything to me. I have work to do." Louie took the box from his brother and started back across the yard.

This was going to be close. While Sparky had been looking at the gray box Uniform Man had gone inside and was talking to Sweetheart at the window trying to explain something to her.

Roscoe and Sparky watched Louie break out of the grass near the deck and sprint for the backpack. He was slowed by the gray box he carried under one arm.

They glanced back at the window and saw Uniform Man gesture for Sweetheart to join him on the deck. He stepped away from the window. She hesitated, wondering if that was the best place for her or if she should continue to watch from the window.

Finally she followed him towards the door to the deck.

"Perfect," Sparky whispered.

"Perfect?" Marvin asked. "What's perfect?"

"You'll see." He answered. Roscoe thought he heard Sparky chuckle.

They turned their attention to Louie. He had the backpack open and was putting the gray box back in place.

The door slid open and Uniform Man followed by Sweetheart stepped out. He must have been explaining how the mutant squirrels work because he had his hands close to his chest and was hopping in a circles around her. Then he threw up his hands and even at the back of the yard they could hear him say, "Poof." He staggered around the deck for a moment and fell. He lay on his back, with his eyes closed and his hands folded across his chest.

Beneath them, under the deck, Louie pulled the cover over the pack and pushed the gray box back into its original place. About the time Uniform Man hit the deck over his head Louie looked up, not sure what was going on above him. Then, knowing he couldn't make it across the yard without being seen, he worked his way to the other side of the deck and waited for the first opportunity to escape.

He'd been so intent on his own safety he hadn't had time to look at the pack. When he'd replaced the gray box it had fallen to one side and the four remaining mutant squirrels had slid out and were lying on the ground.

Uniform Man got up and reached for the butterfly net leaning against the deck rail. He slipped it over his head demonstrating what was in store for the unsuspecting squirrel overcome by the sleeping powder inside the mutants. Roscoe and Marvin watched in horror as he put a finger to his head with his thumb sticking up like he was holding a gun to their head.

He brought his thumb down and said, "Bang."

Sweetheart laughed, clapped her hands then brought them under her chin, dreaming of a yard free of squirrels.

Roscoe could hear Marvin swallow as he thought of the fate that might have been his if Roscoe hadn't pulled him to safety.

"I owe you one Rosc," he whispered.

Roscoe patted him on the shoulder. "You'd have done the same for me."

But Marvin wondered if he would have had enough courage to do it if their roles had been reversed.

Uniform Man walked down the steps of the deck and started to reach for the pack. He paused for a moment. Something was bothering him about its appearance. He looked to see if there were any neighborhood kids around who may have fooled with it while he was gone. When he didn't see anyone he shrugged and started shoving the mutants back in place.

"You've got to do something fast," Sparky told Roscoe. "We can't let him put the mutants back in the pack.

The mutant squirrel Uniform Man had set loose earlier continued its circuit around the yard.

Roscoe nudged Marvin and pointed to the mutant. "He's starting this way, go out and meet him." He gave a nod with his head to indicate the direction Marvin should take.

"Look Roscoe, I'm always glad to help, you know that, but couldn't Jules or somebody else do this instead of me? I mean I've already been out there twice and three times might…"

Roscoe cut him off. "Marvin, it's perfectly safe. Nothing's going to happen to you. Just go out like you did the last time and make sure Uniform Man sees you."

Marvin gave Roscoe one last look that said, "Isn't there some other way?" Seeing no sign that Roscoe was rethinking his decision, Marvin sighed and headed out to meet the approaching mutant.

Sweetheart hollered something to Uniform Man who turned from the pack and looked at the backyard. He nodded to her, saying yes he saw it too, one of the local squirrels had moved into the mutant's path. He dropped down on all fours, and crawled to the edge of the deck dragging the backpack with him.

Sweetheart stood on the deck, close to the rail. She bent slightly at the waist, thinking that would be enough to get her out of sight from the creature in the yard.

"Push the button," Sweetheart yelled at Uniform Man. He started to argue the other squirrel wasn't close enough but before he had a chance to finish what he was going to say, she yanked the gray box out of his hand and aimed it at the mutant.

Poof. She heard something explode and it took her a moment to realize the sound hadn't come from the yard. The mutant continued to move unaffected by the signal form the gray box in her hand.

She pushed the button again. She heard another *poof* but it wasn't from the mutant she was watching who was still cheerfully hopping in it's never changing circle. She pushed it again and heard a third *Poof* this time though the sound was followed by a *thud*.

She looked at the side of the deck and was about to ask why the gray box wasn't working. She let out a shriek and grabbed hold of the deck rail when she saw Uniform Man lying face down in the yard, overcome by the powder from the exploded mutants in the back pack. She glanced at the ground near him and saw the three squirrels he was holding in reserve were blown to pieces.

She saw particles from the exploded mutants falling around her. She turned, thinking she could make it to the door and get inside the house in time to evade the cloud of gas that was slowly moving her way.

She made it to a bench on the deck before she got an odd expression on her face. It looked like she had just told a joke and couldn't figure out why no one was laughing. Then she slowly slid sideways and stretched out on the bench. The gray box fell from her hand to the surface of the deck.

"How long before they come to?" Roscoe asked Sparky.

"Well, they both took a pretty heavy dose of the gas. My guess is, taking their body weight into account and trying to extrapolate…"

Roscoe shook his head. "Just the time Sparky, I don't care what you had to do to figure it out."

"Oh, yea, sorry. I think between 8 and 10 minutes max." Sparky couldn't understand why anyone wouldn't want to know how he came up with the number.

"Grab the mutant Marvin. Check the back, I think there's a switch there." Roscoe was thinking quickly.

Marvin ran across the yard and caught up with the impostor. He felt along it's back until he found the off switch. He pushed it and the mutant stopped with one foot off the ground and one paw raised in the air.

Roscoe and Marvin dragged the mutant over to the feeder and after several minutes, hoisted him to a feeder tube and folded his plastic feet around the wire at the top. When they left it was stretched out, head down, as if getting a seed from the feeder.

Roscoe heard a moan from Uniform Man who was starting to come to.

Roscoe had one more thing to do and he hoped he had enough time for it. He reached Uniform Man's ball cap that had fallen off when his head hit the ground. With quick strokes, using the nails on his paws he removed the red x from the smiling squirrel beneath it.

He dashed up the deck stairs and saw Sweethearts eyes flutter and heard her groan. Carefully he placed the red x across the top of the gray box. Having completed his work he took off for his friends waiting under the tree.

As he got closer he was surprised to see them pointing to a spot in the back yard. They had a look of fear on their faces that caused him to think he'd missed something in his planning.

He turned and saw what had frightened them. A squirrel with a goofy look on his face had left the circle it had followed in the past and was heading toward him. He felt a moment of panic then started to laugh.

"Louie, will you quit goofing around."

Louie kept coming, jumping with mechanical moves until finally diving on top of the helpless, laughing Roscoe. The others broke from the command post and piled on, happy to be part of the victory celebration.

CHAPTER 9

Oh, Oh, Penny Sue

Roscoe rolled from his side to his back. This was his favorite time of day; mid-morning, with his nest still in the shade of the leaves overhead.

He called it, Roscoe time.

He smacked his lips and scratched at a place just below his rib cage

He finally got around to opening one eye and found he was looking directly into the concerned face of Edgar, Chairman of the Committee to Protect Neighborhood Resources.

"She's gone," he said in a whisper. There was no, "Hello," or, "Did you have a pleasant nights sleep," or, "I apologize for bothering you this early." Just a simple, direct, "She's gone."

Roscoe wasn't up to speed. "Who are we talking about here Edgar?" He rubbed his eyes hoping that might help. "Is Edna missing, or is it a…" He ran out of possibilities, it was too early for him to be trying to figure things like this out. He hadn't been to the feeder yet. "He doesn't expect me to be much help on an empty stomach, does he?" He wondered.

"Penny Sue. Who else?" Edgar acted like he couldn't believe he had to explain it to him. Wasn't it obvious? She'd only been staying with him for a few days and this was the second time he'd lost track of her.

At the mention of Penny Sue's name Roscoe became fully awake. "When was she last seen? Did she say anything to anybody about where she was going? Did she leave a note? Is she in the habit of going to the feeder alone? When did you first…"

Edgar waved his paws telling Roscoe to stop. He'd been through the same questions himself and in each case the answer had been no, except for the last one and he wasn't sure when he first noticed she was gone.

Roscoe shot down the tree and into the tall grass that surrounds Seed Man's back yard. He was headed over to Marvin's place thinking they could form a search party when he spotted her at the feeder. He checked the base of the feeder pole and was relieved there was no ferocious dog patrolling the area, nor did he see any sign of the terrible *Squirrel Away Vacuum Box*.

She was sitting on top the feeder with her back to him. There didn't seem to be any effort on her part to leave where she was and cross over to the feeder tubes.

"There you go Edgar, problem solved. She's just out for an early breakfast." Roscoe was pleased he could help lower Edgar's anxiety level. He looked toward him thinking he would say he was eternally grateful for his help or ask if there was anything he could do to show his appreciation.

Instead he saw a look of terror on his face and an arm raised pointing at his granddaughter.

Roscoe looked back and noticed Penny Sue was staring at the big picture window on the back of Seed Man's house. He could see the one they called Uniform Man standing inside, next to Sweetheart. He was the one who had introduced the Community to the mutant squirrels. When his last effort ended so badly the Community had hoped they'd never see him again.

Marvin, who'd just joined them, saw it too. "What is it? What's going on?"

"It's the window Marvin, she sees her reflection in the window." Roscoe answered with out taking his eyes off her.

Edgar gripped his paws tightly. "Vanity. Oh, vanity." He hung his head and stared at the ground. "Thy name is disaster."

"Take it easy Edgar, we can figure something out." Roscoe tried to console him but stopped when he saw Uniform Man step away from the window, "He's coming outside, I've got to…" He stopped speaking when he saw the back door slide open and Uniform Man step onto the deck.

Without saying a word, Roscoe sprinted across the yard to the feeder. He made it to the support pole as Uniform Man reached the last step on the deck. He was up the pole in a second and spoke quietly to Penny Sue. "We've have to go now, we don't have much time." He looked over his shoulder to check on Uniform Man's progress.

It was obvious Penny Sue was unaware of the confusion going on around her. She couldn't take her eyes off her reflection.

"I'm beautiful, Roscoe. I can see myself in the window and I'm beautiful." She didn't seem able to look away.

"We can talk about that later Penny Sue, but first we've got to get out of here. Uniform Man is…"

While Roscoe was trying to get Penny Sue to turn away from the window, Uniform Man lifted the pole with the net on the end of it and brought it down over the top of the feeder sealing off any chance they had of escaping. He turned his wrist quickly and flipped the bag over catching them by surprise and leaving them upside down in the bottom of the net.

With his other hand he pulled back the folds of a black, leather bag and dropped the net with the squirrels in it.

Roscoe heard a zip and the last thing he saw before the source of light at the top of the bag went out was Sweetheart, still at the window, clapping her hands and smiling.

He heard Penny Sue whimper.

Roscoe patted her shoulder and said, "We're going to be okay, I'll think of something, don't worry." He wished he felt as confident as he was trying to sound.

The bag they were in swung back and forth; Roscoe figured they were being carried someplace. They were thrown roughly in the back of Uniform Man's truck. Roscoe heard a yelp from Penny Sue about the same time the truck door slammed shut and the engine started.

"You okay?" Roscoe whispered.

"I think so," she answered bravely, but there was something in her voice that told him she wasn't.

They bumped along in the back of the truck. Roscoe tried to count, to get some idea how long they'd been traveling but each time he started the bag would slide across the bed of the truck and slam into the side. By the time he checked to see if Penny Sue was okay, he'd lost track of the count and had to start over.

Finally they stopped. Uniform Man picked up the bag they were in and carried it a few steps. To Roscoe's amazement, he set the bag on the ground, unzipped the top and turned them loose. They took off toward the trees. Penny Sue must have hurt her ankle during the ride in the truck because she was limping badly.

By the time they got to safety Roscoe looked back and noticed Uniform Man had changed the sign on his truck from, *Squirrels Away* to *Fire Away Squirrel Hunting-No Limit*. He wondered what the difference was.

He heard the truck drive off had no idea where they were; it was impossible to tell how far they'd traveled. Sliding around in the bed of the truck had thrown off his natural sense of direction, he had no idea how to get back to their Community.

He heard Penny Sue sniff as she fought back tears. "We're not going to make it back are we?" Her voice jerked along and her words were almost lost as she spoke between sobs and tears.

Roscoe put his arm around her shoulder. "Don't worry, we'll work something out, I've been in worse situations than this before." He knew he had to put up a brave front to keep her from going over the edge and becoming depressed. There was some truth in what he'd said about being in difficult spots before but they had been in his old Neighborhood where he knew his way around and had friends to help him out.

This was something completely different, he was on his own.

While he was thinking about their situation and comforting Penny Sue he saw movement farther back in the trees. "Hello," he called out, "is someone there?"

He heard the rustling of leaves and could barely make out the shape of another squirrel. He had a branch full of leaves strapped to his back and his face and paws were covered with mud.

"We're new here, but you probably know that." Roscoe felt he must have sounded pretty stupid saying they were new to the area and decide to start over. "Ah, I'm Roscoe and this is Penny Sue. Do you have a name or a nick name or…" The silence from the other squirrel bothered him.

"Duck," the camouflaged squirrel said.

"What did you say your name…" Before he could ask if he'd heard him right the bark of a tree limb above his head exploded into sawdust. He and Penny Sue looked around, desperate for a new place to hide but before they could move the squirrel hidden in the leaves said, "Duck again."

Roscoe couldn't figure him out. If his name was Duck, why didn't he just come forward and say, "Hello my name is…" *Kaboom*, the ground a few feet from him shot in the air covering both he and Penny Sue with a light coating of dirt.

"Oh boy," Roscoe could hear the other squirrel say. He ran over to them following a zigzag path. Even when he was close Roscoe had trouble seeing him, he blended into the surroundings so well.

He muttered something about rookies and then said, "Follow me before you get yourselves shot." Then he turned and ran the same odd pattern back into the trees.

"Do you think we should go?" Penny Sue asked as she watched him disappear into the tall grass.

"I don't know." Roscoe was trying to make sense of everything that had happened to them since Uniform Man opened the sack and turned them loose. "It could be a tr…" **Ka Whamm**, a large hole opened up in the trunk of the tree next to him.

They took off following as closely as possible the route they'd seen the mysterious squirrel take.

Once they got into the tall grass, Roscoe looked around. "I'm sure he came in here but I don't…"

A branch moved and the stranger walked towards them. He stopped when he was in front of Roscoe. He stared at the two of them for a moment and then gave a quick nod of his head and

The Squirrel Chronicles: Book One

the foliage behind him moved to form a circle around them.

Roscoe blinked trying to figure out what was going on.

"Rule number one around here, that is if you want to stay alive and I'm guessing you do, is keep your head down." He walked away from them and stared into space. He turned around. "Rule number two you've got to get something to cover you up. You'll need the leaf and mud pack, which I've got on sale this week for two and a half nuts each which in your case will be a total of five nuts. Am I right Rodney?"

A voice behind him said, "That's correct boss."

Before Rodney could finish the first squirrel started talking again. "On top of that your going to need a place to stay, that's going to run you another nut a week. Then to attend my seminar on *Surviving the Hunter*, which I heartily recommend, is going to run you each another nut and a half. Which brings us to a grand total of..." He looked in the tree limbs above Roscoe's head and waited.

"That would be a total of nine nuts boss," a voice, Roscoe assumed was Rodney spoke through the leaves.

"Excellent Rod, nine nuts it is." He looked Roscoe and Penny Sue over. "But, you look like a nice couple. Tell you what, I'll let you have the whole package for eight nuts, what do you say to that?"

"Look," Roscoe took a step toward him. "We were kidnapped and dropped off here. We didn't bring any nuts with us. In fact, we didn't have time to bring anything." He looked at Penny Sue who nodded in agreement. "You can search us if you want. Besides I don't know who you are or where we are or..."

"I'm Geezer, my friends call me Geez and your in a heavily wooded area that is crawling with hunters who's sole ambition in life is terminate yours." He'd leaned into Roscoe as he talked and then backed off. "That's your situation in a nutshell."

The three squirrels stood for a moment not knowing what to say. Then Roscoe said, "Suppose we decide to go it alone."

About the time Roscoe finished his question another squirrel broke through the circle of protection and announced, "We've got a live one at five o'clock Geez."

Geezer looked at the speaker and told him to, "Get the demonstration model ready." The squirrel nodded and slipped away.

Geezer turned toward Roscoe and said, "If you'll direct your attention to the tree limb over there." He pointed to a spot high in the branches of a tree about twenty feet away. They watched as the one who moments before delivered the message about a live one at five o'clock, slid the replica of a squirrel made out of mud across a tree limb until it locked snugly into a place where the limb split. When he finished he looked in their direction and gave a quick wave with his paw then turned and disappeared from view.

Roscoe could hear the crunching of leaves beneath them as a hunter stepped slowly into a small clearing, turning his head from side to side, searching tree limbs for wildlife. When he spotted the mud squirrel he raised the rifle to his shoulder, took aim and pulled the trigger. The blast was deafening and when Roscoe and Penny Sue had recovered enough to look the mud squirrel as well as the branch holding it were gone.

The hunter poked what was left of the mud squirrel with the barrel of his rifle then walked out of the clearing.

Roscoe looked back at Geezer. "Maybe we can work something out."

"Hey I like you kids, okay. You remind me a lot of me and the misses when we were starting out. So, I'll tell you what I'm going to do. I'm going to give you the whole package, branch and mud kit, a place to stay, admittance to the seminar and I'll throw in a subscription to the Internest early warning system for seven nuts. Take it or leave it."

"I guess we don't have a choice but what's the Internest?" Roscoe was puzzled, he'd never heard of it before.

"We've wired all the nests. A hunter enters the woods and a red light comes on telling you to stay put. When the green light comes on your free to move about the woods." He talked like it was no big deal. Roscoe made a mental note to pass the idea on to Sparky if and when the made it back home. The Community of Abner wasn't bothered by hunters but he thought it could have other uses.

"Any questions?" He waited a second and when neither Roscoe or Penny Sue said anything he continued. "No? Okay then I'll have Rodney take you…" Geezer looked them over wanting to make sure the understood the details of their agreement.

"We don't plan to be hear too long, eventually we want to get back to our Neighborhood." Roscoe thought it was important to fill Geezer in on what he was thinking, he didn't want him to get the idea this was a permanent situation.

"Ah, then let me tell you about the *Geezer Escape Service*. Another nut from each of you and I'll guarantee you'll be on your way home in a week." He raised his eyebrows encouraging an answer from them.

"We'll think about it. Thanks Geez." Roscoe turned and motioned for Rodney to take them to their nest.

The days flew by as Roscoe and Penny Sue divided their time between gathering nuts to pay for all the services Geezer provided and trying to avoid getting shot by hunters who roamed through the woods.

One morning they were out looking for nuts when they ran into Rodney. "Hey Rodney. When's that boss of yours going to come up with a plan to get us home?" There was a note of frustration in Roscoe's voice, they'd been away from their Community a lot longer than he'd planned.

"Why don't you ask him?" Rodney stepped aside and Geezer seemed to appear out of nowhere. As he approached Roscoe the space in the circle he'd left was quickly filled in by someone else in his group. They formed the same circle of camouflaged protection they had when Geezer first talked to them.

"You've got a question about the escape service? If I'm not mistaken you didn't subscribe." As he approached Roscoe wondered if he could ever get used to squirrels in camouflage outfits.

"Hey Geezer, I'm sorry, I didn't mean to be…" Roscoe started to apologize but Geezer cut him off.

"For get about it. You, of all people, know a good plan takes awhile to come together. Am I right?" He looked at Roscoe, his paws open towards him.

"Well, yeah, but I didn't see any signs you were doing anything or…"

"Let's get to the point. Rodney you want to set the scene for us?" Geezer stepped to one side and Rodney cleared a place in the dirt in front of him then started drawing as he talked.

"The assailant, AKA Uniform Man, has been here three times this week. The first time at 0800 hours, the second at…"

Geezer interrupted. "He's been here three times this week, that's all we need to know, at the moment the times of the visits aren't important." He looked at Rodney and motioned for him to continue.

"0945 hours." Rodney was having trouble letting go of his

prepared presentation. "He, ah, three times, okay." He drew an aerial view of the neighborhood. "He always pulls in and parks here." He drew what looked like a box with two wheels on each side to represent Uniform Man's truck. "He gets out of the drivers door, walks around and picks up the bag in back."

He drew an X behind the truck to indicate where Uniform Man stood when he took the bag out of the truck. "He proceeds around this way and approaches the drop area." He drew a series of dashes in the dirt to indicate the path he took from the truck to the drop area.

"He opens the bag, releases the captives, and returns to the truck." More dashes followed his path back to the truck. "He throws the empty bag in the back, gets in the drivers side, backs up," he paused for a moment letting his last comment sink in. "And, drives away."

"Were any from our Community? Abner? Have there been some we know out here in the…" Roscoe straightened up, ready to dash into the tree's to find out who else had been taken from Seed Man's yard.

"Our interviews with the new arrivals indicate," Rodney flipped through a small notebook, stopping at each sheet long enough to look at the information on it. "None from Abner."

Roscoe's shoulders dropped. For just a moment he thought one of his buddies had come to help him. Then he remembered they had no idea where he was, they'd just seen he and Penny Sue being carried away.

"I always say, dance with the one that brought you." Geezer moved along side Rodney and they both looked at Roscoe thinking he'd get the clue and say, "Aha."

"I don't get it. Who said anything about dancing?" Roscoe was puzzled. The comment made no sense but the two in front of him seemed to think it was the absolute right thing to say.

"He puts the bag in the back of the truck, gets in and backs up. Every time." Rodney spoke slowly thinking he'd gone to fast the first time he said it.

"So…?" Roscoe wasn't there yet, he was missing something important but didn't know what it was.

"Dance with the one who brought you." Geezer nodded as he spoke.

"See, I'm not making the conn…" Roscoe stopped. He straightened. He looked off in the distance. "We need to be in that bag when he leaves don't we?"

Geezer and Rodney smiled and nodded. "And we have just the plan that will buy the two of you enough time get in it." Geezer directed their attention to the drawing on the dirt in front of them. "He goes around here," he drew a line from the back of the truck to the door. "You come in here," he drew another line from the edge of the woods to the back of the truck. "But, before that, while he's unloading the contents of his bag over here, we put a rock behind the front wheel here." He drew a small object in back of the wheel on the passengers side of the sketch." He has to get out of the truck and remove the rock which gives you enough time to handle any problem you might run into while trying to get into the bag. Maybe it's zipped closed. Maybe it's inside out. Who knows? But a little extra time won't hurt."

Rodney nodded in agreement.

"How do we know he'll go back to our neighborhood? You just said none of the latest deliveries were from there." Roscoe liked the plan, and having been confronted with similar problems in the past he appreciated the preparation that had gone into this one. But, they could end up anywhere; maybe someplace worse than where they are now.

The Squirrel Chronicles: Book One

"Hey, I said we'd get you out I didn't say we could guarantee you'd end up in your old Community. We can stall him long enough to get you in the bag, that's as far as the guarantee goes." Geezer gestured the decision to go or not was up to Roscoe.

It didn't take Roscoe long to decide what to do. He whispered something to Penny Sue who shook her head yes.

"We'll go with your plan and take our chances." Roscoe rubbed his paws together anxious to get on with it. He realized the thing that was bothering him and putting him in such a bad mood was that he hadn't been able to figure a way out of the woods on his own. Now he had to go along with someone else's plan. Even thought it sounded like they'd just come up with the plan he had a feeling they weren't the first to use it.

Geezer looked pleased. "Did I mention there's a small fee for placing the rock behind the tire. Say, a nut each." He was surprised by the look on Roscoe's face. He quickly added, "Hey, it's business okay, it's not personal."

Now all they had to do was wait until Uniform Man made another delivery.

It didn't take long, a couple of days, enough time for Roscoe and Penny Sue to gather enough nuts to cover the placement of the rock under the tire of the truck and pay off the last of what they owed on the *Geezer Escape Service* fee.

The plan worked to perfection, just like it had been outlined on the ground. After depositing his latest victims, Uniform Man walked back to the truck and tossed the bag in the back. He started the motor and tried to back up but couldn't make it over the rock. By the time he removed it, Roscoe and Penny Sue were inside the bag. Roscoe left part of it open so he could look around as Uniform Man drove away.

The first two places he stopped were false alarms. Roscoe

gave him enough time to move away from the truck before poking his head out of the opening and looking around for something familiar. Apparently Uniform Man didn't have any luck catching wildlife at either stop. The minute they got close to their Neighborhood Roscoe knew where they were. For one thing the air took on a different smell and for another the tree branches he could see from his place in the truck bed looked familiar; they'd been his playground as he was growing up.

"Get ready," he whispered to Penny Sue, "when the truck stops I want you out of the bag and over the side as fast as possible. Okay?"

It was too dark to see but he guessed she'd nodded yes.

When they finally stopped, Roscoe pulled the zipper on top of the bag open a little wider and squeezed out. He felt a sense of panic when he heard the truck door slam shut and Uniform Man's footsteps move toward them instead of away as he had at the other stops.

Penny Sue was half way out of the bag when she stopped and looked at Roscoe. "Some of my fur is caught in the…" She couldn't think of the word zipper and as she heard Uniform Man getting closer she couldn't think of anything, she froze, unable to move.

Roscoe saw the top of Uniform Man's cap moving along the side of the truck. He was whistling and snapping his fingers as he rounded the back and stopped. Something in the bed of the truck caught his eye. He stepped forward, put his arms on the tailgate and saw Penny Sue, half in and half out of the leather bag.

Before he could figure out what to do, Roscoe dashed from the corner of the truck bed and dove for the latch on the zipper. It pulled open enough for Penny Sue to get out and slip over the side of the truck.

The Squirrel Chronicles: Book One

Uniform Man didn't know whether to try to grab her or stay put and take care of the one still in the back of the truck.

Roscoe waited for him to move one way or the other. As soon as he did, raising one leg to lift himself over the tailgate of the truck, Roscoe went over the opposite side, but not before grabbing the bag in his teeth and taking it with him.

Uniform Man stood in the back of the truck and watched him disappear into the tall grass. He turned to check the picture window and saw Sweetheart. She'd been watching from the time he backed his truck into the driveway to the last of the squirrels jumping over the side. Her arms were folded across her chest and she shook her head from side to side as if to say, "How could you allow two dumb animals to out smart you?"

She gave him one last withering look then turned and walked away from the window.

Meanwhile, Roscoe and Penny Sue dashed through the tall grass and ran passed surprised Community members waiting in line for their turn at the feeder. When it finally dawned on them who they were they hollered, "Welcome back," and, "Where in the world have you kids been?"

Roscoe's plan was to take Penny Sue to Edgar's nest as quickly as he could. He could imagine how miserable her grandfather had been, thinking he was partly to blame for getting Penny Sue in the predicament she was in.

They were about to start up Edgar's tree when Roscoe happened to glance into the Committee meeting room and saw him, sitting in a chair, hunched over and staring at the floor.

He'd been so consumed with guilt he hadn't bothered to light the candle on his desk.

Roscoe pushed open the door and gestured for Penny Sue to go in and tell him she was back.

"Grandpa," was all she got out before tears took over. She knew if she tried to say something else it would only make matters worse.

Edgar straightened in his chair and turned towards her. She was surprised by his appearance; there were dark circles under his eyes and even in the dimly lit room she could see he'd lost weight.

"Penny Sue? Is that..." When it finally dawned on him she was back he leapt from his chair, ran across the room and hugged her. They both tried to talk between sobs of joy at seeing one another.

"Where have you been? When I saw Uniform Man drive away with you in the back of his truck I was sure I'd never see you ag..." The thought of never seeing her again produced a new round of tears.

"But what a clever young squirrel you are to have found your way back." Edgar stepped away, holding her paws in his, checking to make sure she was all right.

"Actually it was Roscoe who..." She tried to explain what happened, how Roscoe risked his life to set her free but Edgar shook his head.

"We won't mention that name again will we? Why, at the first sign of danger he took off and hasn't been seen since." Edgar turned and looked out of the small window in the room. "From now on, the less you see of him the better off you'll be."

"No, grandpa, you don't understand. Ros..." Was as far as she got before Edgar took her arm and said, "I'm sure your tired and hungry. Run up to the nest and I'll get some seeds for you." Edgar stepped out of the meeting room and headed for the feeder.

When he saw Edgar leave the meeting room and head for the feeder, Roscoe stepped into the shadow of a tree so he couldn't be seen.

Penny Sue walked outside, looking for him. When he stepped from behind the tree she ran over and hugged him. "I tried to tell him it was you who saved my life but he wouldn't listen."

Roscoe shook his head, "Don't worry about it, it'll all get worked out." She kissed him on the cheek and left for Edgar's nest. For a moment he wondered if Geezer had a *How to Explain Everything Once You Get Back Home* service. He decided if he did, he probably couldn't afford it.

Penny Sue called his name and when he turned around she said, "Thank you Roscoe. I…well…thanks."

She turned and headed up the tree.

"Me to," he whispered. Roscoe watched her until she went over the side of the nest. She stopped, looked down and blew him a kiss.

He reached out and acted like he caught it. "Good night sweet…" he started to say, "heart," but stopped when he saw Edgar return to the Clearing.

"Roscoe what are you doing here?" There was a disgusted sound to Edgar's voice.

"Oh, me, I, well, ah…" Roscoe didn't know what to say.

"Penny Sue made it back from whatever awful place Uniform Man took her. No thanks to you, I might add." Edgar had seeds in both paws and didn't want to spend anymore time with Roscoe than he had to.

"We need to have a long talk sometime about having courage in the face of danger and rising above your own self interest to think of the safety of others." There was a stern quality to Edgar's voice. "That will be all for now Roscoe. My granddaughter needs me." Edgar dismissed Roscoe and started climbing his tree.

Roscoe took one last glance at Edgar's nest. All he could see of Penny Sue was the top of her head, her eyes and mouth.

She winked and he thought she mouthed the words, "I love you." He wasn't sure, maybe it was, "Thank you," or, "Are you okay?"

As he walked to his nest he decided he was right the first time, she'd said she loved him.

CHAPTER 10

It's Not Always About the Seeds

Roscoe felt miserable.

He'd been walking around the base of his tree all night. At some point a cold front had moved in bringing with it rain and a sudden drop in temperature.

He was cold, wet and tired.

The thing he couldn't figure out was why, out of all the nests in the Community, Pete O'Malley kept picking his. Pete's the local bully with no real Community of his own. He goes from Neighborhood to Neighborhood causing trouble and like Roscoe had experienced too many times, delights in throwing perfectly respectable, peace loving members of the Community out of their nests for the night.

There's never an announcement that he's coming so the victim never has an opportunity to make arrangements with friends. He just shows up and takes over.

He heard scraping sounds overhead, looked up and watched Pete work his way down the tree. His coat was dark and he wore his fur longer than everyone else in the Community. When he spoke Roscoe had to strain to listen because he never talked louder than a whisper. His voice was surprisingly high pitched for someone his size and each word sounded like it had been squeezed through a narrow tube before finally reaching day light.

"Youse got a little clean up work to do in youse nest, Rosc." Pete never looks at who he's talking to, instead, he faces the opposite direction with his back toward them. "Me and Stubs had a few friends over and, what can I say, things got a little out of control. If youse knows what I'm talking about."

Pete's buddy Stubs followed him down the tree and chose to stand next to Roscoe. He smiled and nodded when he heard what Pete said.

Roscoe didn't know what to say so, for once in his life, he kept his mouth shut. He'd heard stories about those who said the wrong thing when talking to Pete and regretted it later.

"Youse listening to what I'm sayin here Rosc?" Pete stared off in the distance waiting for an answer.

"Yes," Roscoe muttered and shook his head, a gesture wasted on Pete. All he could think about was climbing into his nest and getting some sleep, now he finds out they left it in a mess.

He was thinking so hard about the condition of his nest and how miserable he felt he almost didn't hear what Pete said next.

"Did I miss something there Stubby?" There was a long silence after he spoke.

"I don't think so boss." Stubs wasn't sure what Pete was talking about. He thought he was asking if they'd left something in Roscoe's nest. He started to say he'd looked around before he came down and hadn't seen anything but stopped when Pete continued.

"Was Yes, all I heard? Was that it? Just yes?" The question hung in the air. Roscoe shivered. Stubs scratched his head.

"Yea, boss, he said yes, but, oh, oh, I see where youse is going wid dis. Youse is looking for dem three magic letters." Stubs smiled, pleased he'd figured out what Pete was talking about.

"Yes sir." They didn't have to spell it out for Roscoe. It was bad enough he'd taken his nest for the night, now he was trying to humiliate him.

"Much better, Roscy. I'm sure youse will remember dem same words de nex time me and Stubbs pays youse a visit." Pete shrugged his shoulders and he and Stubs began their slow walk across the Clearing toward Seed Man's yard.

"Next time?" Roscoe said to himself. Pete's parting comment was the last straw to fall on his weary shoulders and it felt like it weighed a ton.

Roscoe could see other members of the Community draw back as Pete and Stubs strolled past. They tried to find a tree or shrub to put between themselves and Pete's menacing glare.

Marvin and Jules were headed to the feeder, talking about something that

happened during the night, when they spotted Pete their conversation stopped and they froze in place looking like two lawn ornaments.

When Pete and Stubs were safely out of the yard Marvin and Jules came over to Roscoe and asked what that was all about.

"You know them," Roscoe sneezed. His head was stopped up and his body ached. "See ya guys." Roscoe worked his way up his tree. He had to stop several times; once to sneeze and a second time to catch his breath.

When he finally reached his nest his heart sank. One side of it was almost gone and the bottom was so thin you could see the ground through it. There wasn't enough support left to hold a small bird let alone a fully grown squirrel.

Marvin climbed up and stood next to him. "Wow, what happened? Did the storm do this?"

"Yeah, you could say that. I think it was called Hurricane Pete," Roscoe leaned against a tree branch to rest. He was thinking it would take hours to get things back in place and all he wanted to do at the moment was lie down.

"Why don't you go over to my place? Jules and I will fix things up. You're not in any condition for this kind of work." When Marvin didn't get an answer he looked and saw his friend Roscoe leaning against a tree branch, sound asleep.

When word got out about Roscoe's problem everyone in the Community pitched in and gathered enough material to fill in the empty places in his nest. Several skilled in weaving twigs and branches together eventually got his nest back in better condition than before Pete arrived.

When they were finished, Marvin guided Roscoe from the tree limb to his nest and helped him lie down and then quietly left.

There is no sleep like the sleep of an exhausted squirrel. Roscoe didn't wake up until late in the afternoon. When he did, he discovered his friends had placed a small pile of seeds close by. He ate them, rolled over and went back to sleep.

The next morning he was feeling better.

He was hungry, which he took to be a good sign so he climbed down the tree intending to go straight to the squirrel feeder. Instead he discovered he'd landed in the middle of a meeting of the Committee To Protect Neighborhood Resources.

"Quite a little sleep you had there Roscoe." Edgar, Chairman of the Committee said. "We've been waiting here for some time." His front paws were locked behind his back and he paced back and forth as he spoke.

Roscoe started to say something sarcastic, he wasn't in the mood to be hassled by anyone else and was still angry about what Pete had done. But, before he could say anything, he saw his friend Darrin shake his head no.

Since he didn't get an apology, Edgar continued. "We, that is, the whole Community heard about your, ah, unfortunate little problem with you-know-who and some, that is most of us feel, we…"

"For heavens sake Edgar will you just come out and say it." One of the Committee members stepped forward. "We think we can come up with a plan that will prevent this kind of thing from happening again."

"You're going to come up with a plan? For me?" Roscoe wasn't sure what the speaker was getting at but he knew any plan developed by the Committee was doomed for failure. He'd seen them spring into action before; taking weeks discussing the problem before coming up with something resembling a plan. Then more time was required to review and vote on it.

"Think about it Roscoe, the last three times Pete has visited our Community he's stayed at your place and left it in a mess." Edgar resumed his pacing. "Do you see a pattern here? Isn't it obvious Pete has discovered you're a push over? A cream puff? A…"

"I think he gets the picture," another member of the Committee interrupted.

"We can pool our resources," Edgar continued, ignoring the comment.

"We can provide a united front," someone added.

"We can pool our resources," a third pitched in, apparently unaware that Edgar had already said it.

"All for one," Edgar stuck his out his paw.

"One for all," a committee member put his paw on top of Edgar's.

They waited for others to join them. When they didn't, the dropped their arms and looked embarrassed.

"Oh no," Roscoe got a frightened look on his face and pointed toward Seed Man's yard. "I think Pete's coming back."

"Back?" Edgar shouted over his shoulder as he took off for the Clearing.

"To our Community?" another asked as he shot up a tree trunk and disappeared in the branches.

"Now?" The third ran around in circles until he finally dove under a shrub at the edge of the yard.

"That's what I thought," Roscoe mumbled then waved his arms and said, "just kidding."

Slowly, the Committee members left their hiding places and came back to join him.

"That was very unprofessional Roscoe," the one who'd climbed the tree was rubbing his elbow where he'd bumped it in his hurry to get away.

"Totally unnecessary," the second one added as he brushed dirt from his knees.

"You caught us off guard," Edgar offered as an excuse but he kept looking around, studying the edges of the yard in case Roscoe wasn't kidding and Pete had decided to return.

"But I think it proves my point." Roscoe looked at the ground for a moment than back at those around him. "I appreciate your offer to help gentlemen, but there are some things one has to take care of oneself and," he waited a moment, making sure they understood he was serious. "This is one of those things."

He looked at each of them for a moment then turned and walked away.

"You're probably right Roscoe," Edgar called after him. "I remember years ago I had a similar ex…"

"Give it a rest Edgar," a Committee member put a paw on his shoulder, "he's too far away to hear you. Besides, that story of yours is getting old."

Roscoe sighed as he walked to the feeder. He couldn't figure out why Pete kept picking his nest when he came to the Community. He'd been afraid of him since his first day of seed school where he'd watched in horror as he pushed his friends around. Then, one fall afternoon, he turned on him.

"Maybe the Committee is right," he told himself. "Maybe I am a push over."

After a quick snack he made his way up his tree and took his usual position when doing serious thinking, lying with his stomach pressed against the bottom of the nest and his chin resting on the rim.

Pfft. Pfft. Pfft.

Roscoe stuck his head up and looked over the side of his nest and, when he didn't see anything unusual, returned to his thinking position.

Pfft. Pfft. Pfft.

How could anyone do any serious thinking with that noise in the background, he wondered. He sat up and looked above him but everything seemed normal. When he finally looked down he discovered the source of the noise; Seed Man had turned on his lawn sprinkler.

He settled back in his nest trying to concentrate on the problem at hand, he figured it wouldn't be long before Pete returned and he had to have a plan in place when he did. The sound of the sprinkler kept interrupting his thoughts.

He was about to give up and do something else when the first piece of an idea broke loose from a corner of his mind and floated into view. The sprinkler that had been such an irritation earlier actually provided the first part of the answer to the *O'Malley Problem* and with each *Pfft*, new ideas joined the first one and gradually arranged themselves into a plan.

He scrambled down his tree but before heading for the first place on his list he took a quick detour through the water coming from the sprinkler. "Thank you. Thank you. Thank you," he said as he danced under the falling drops.

He found his friend Yardley where he thought he would, leaning against the trunk of a tree and flipping through the pages of his notebook.

"Hey Yardley, how's it going?" Roscoe tried to sound casual, he didn't want to tip him off too early about the vital role he'd play in his plan to get even with Pete.

"Oh, hey Roscoe." Yardley barely looked up from his notebook; he was busy studying a diagram that covered most of the page.

"I suppose you heard about Pete and me?"

Yardley looked up and blinked. "No, not really. Well sure, I mean, who hasn't?" He shrugged and said, "Could you excuse me for a moment Roscoe? I'm, ah, you know." He gestured with his head at the notebook in his hand.

"Sure, no problem," Roscoe took a step back. Yardley had no idea it was the information in his notebook that interested Roscoe.

He watched as Yardley, after a quick glance at the diagram, lined himself up with the edge of Seed Man's house, checked to make sure he was even with the rose bush, then made four jumps toward the house, turned right and made three smaller ones. He disappeared beneath the tall grass at the edge of the yard for a moment then popped up holding an acorn in one paw.

He came back alongside Roscoe and began nibbling around the edge of the nut while he made a note in his book. "You can't beat acorns that have been in the ground all winter."

He angled the nut to one side and offered Roscoe a bite.

"No thanks Yardley but, out of curiosity, how many acorns do you think you've got buried out there?" Roscoe gestured toward the field in back of Seed Man's yard.

Yardley flipped to the last page in his notebook. "Looks like, if I don't count this one, 639." He closed the notebook and resumed eating.

"I wonder if you'd be interested in helping me out?" Roscoe put an arm around his shoulder and explained the part he'd play in the plan to teach Pete and Stubs a lesson.

When he finished Yardley had only one question. "Will I get them all back?"

"I guarantee it," Roscoe answered and patted him on the back.

His next stop took him to the big rock that separates the Community of Abner from the Community of Ben. He was never sure which tree Homer was working in so he had to look up through the branches for his sign. He finally spotted, *"Quality Nest Repair by Homer,"* and climbed up to see if he was around.

He found him deep inside an abandoned nest looking for useable pieces of material before tearing it down. Homer spoke without looking up. "I didn't think I'd see you this soon. We just patched up your nest, what was it, two or three days ago?"

"Yea, and I really appreciate what you guys did. But, this is about another issue." While Roscoe talked he pulled a piece of paper from his back pocket and unfolded it.

Homer stood up, stretched and joined Roscoe where the light was better. He looked the paper over, hummed a little then added a few notes of his own to the sketch. "See, that's the only way it's going to work. You've got to do something with the corner branches here and here." He pointed to the additions he'd made to the drawing.

"But, it can be done? What I've drawn here?" Roscoe appreciated Homer's comments but didn't want to discover after all his work he'd come up with something that couldn't be built.

"Oh sure," Homer nodded. "I don't see why anyone would want to do it but, yes, it will work."

"How quickly do you think you could get on this Homer? I mean, I'm in a real time crunch."

"How about I bring my crew by this afternoon? That soon enough for you?" Homer smiled. He'd figured out why Roscoe needed the modifications to his nest and understood why he was in such a hurry to get the work done.

"I owe you Homer." Roscoe couldn't believe he'd be able to get on it so quickly.

It took him awhile to find Marvin and Jules. He told them what was going on and after several questions they split up, each anxious to checkout their part in the plan.

After grabbing some seeds from the feeder and taking a quick nap under a shrub at the back of Seed Man's yard, Roscoe headed back to his nest, determined to spend the evening reviewing every detail of his plan; it had come together so quickly he knew there was a chance he'd forgotten something.

It was nearly dark when he stepped off the path and took the short cut to his nest. He was thinking so hard about his plan he didn't notice the figure leaning against the trunk of his tree.

"Well, well, look what de cat's drug in." Stubs spoke as he pushed himself away from the tree. "Looks like youse going to be spending a little quality time on the ground tonight there Roscy. Petey has a few friends over and as soon as I square things away wit youse, I'm going to join him."

"Oh no. You mean Pete is back?" Roscoe said it as loud as he could. It was dark and he had no idea if his friends had been able to get things in place or not. He thought he'd have at least a week before Pete returned.

"I'm right here Rosc, youse don't needs to be shouting or nothing like dat. I just hope the boss didn't hear youse. If he did it would mean big troubles for youse my friend and I'm talking big troubles." Stubs looked up and listened in case Pete asked him what was going on.

"Okay Stubs. I get it. Hee Hee." Roscoe didn't know what else to do to let his friends know Pete was back. He put his paw on the tree trying to look as casual as possible but mostly hoping it would keep his legs from shaking so badly.

"Youse is standing on my last nerve there Roscy. I'm telling youse knock it off." Stubs shoved Roscoe to one side and started up the tree. "I don't wants to hear no peeps out youse from now on, got it?"

Roscoe nodded yes he got it. When he'd put his paw on the tree he thought he'd felt something. Now that Stubs was out of sight he reached up and worked his way around the trunk, feeling carefully for the piece of rope he'd touched earlier.

He finally found it, Homer had wrapped the end of the rope around a rusty nail someone had driven half way in the trunk years before. Roscoe waited until he was sure Stubs was in the nest before he unwound the rope.

He wished he knew where every body was, it was dark and

he was having trouble separating normal night sounds from those his friends would make getting ready for their part in the plan.

He decided to wait a little longer. He heard laughter overhead and once, the sound of a bottle falling on the ground startled him.

He made up his mind this had to be it ready or not.

He wound the end of the rope tightly around his paw and yanked.

An awful silence followed the pull. What if Homer had been wrong about the location of the hinges? Or, what if one of his workers had failed to cut a branch they were supposed to? All he could think of at the moment were all of the things that could go wrong.

But for once in his brief career of coming up with farfetched schemes none of them did.

He heard the floor of his nest give way and come to rest hanging toward the ground by the two big hinges Homer had added to the sketch.

The silence was broken by screams from Pete, Stubs and their three friends. They hit the ground with a thud; two of them landing on top of Pete and momentarily knocking the breath out of him.

Stubs, the first to recover, spun around to defend himself. He spotted Roscoe. "If I find out youse was behind this so help me I'll…"

Pfft. Pfft. Pfft. Roscoe heard the sprinkler come on telling him that Marvin and Jules had done their job. Marvin was supposed to move the sprinkler close to his tree and Jules was to open the faucet when he heard Pete and Stubs hit the ground. It wasn't long before huge drops of water began pouring down on Pete and his friends. It made the grass slick and caused them to fall several times as they tried to make their way out of the big circle of water cast by the sprinkler.

Roscoe smiled. He hadn't been sure if there'd been enough time for Jules to make it to the hydrant at the back of Seed Man's house.

Pete and his friends were soaked. They stumbled around and knocked each other down as they tried to find a path that led away from the water.

They finally made it to dry ground and stopped outside the edge of the arc the sprinkler could reach.

Pete said something to Stubs who was trying to scrape the grass and mud off his back. They both turned and looked at Roscoe.

Roscoe shrugged his shoulders and pushed his paws in the air giving them a look that said, "Who? Me involved? No way."

It didn't take a genius to see they weren't buying it.

Pete was surrounded by his friends, his lips were moving but Roscoe couldn't make out what he was saying. He held a paw to his ear and said, "What? I'm sorry. I can't hear you. You're going to have to speak up." He had to keep them in that exact spot a moment longer.

Pete stopped talking when he heard what sounded like a rope coming loose. It made a zipping sound as the main string on the net Yardley had hung overhead came loose. Pete and his guests looked up in time to see nuts, 639 of them to be exact, falling towards them.

One of the quests dove out of the way and only received minor bruises. Stubs made any effort to reach out and protect his boss but was too late; Pete took the full brunt of the falling nuts.

Roscoe could hear squeals coming from under the pile of nuts.

It took awhile before the acorns began to slide off as Pete and the others tried to stand. They staggered, and stumbled over the nuts before they got away from the drop area.

Roscoe watched them look around, trying to remember where they were before the nuts fell. When they finally found him he could see Pete lift his arm and point his way. You didn't have to be skilled lip reader to understand that Pete told Stubs to, "Get him."

Roscoe had reached the end of his plan. He'd foolishly hoped falling from his nest and getting pummeled with nuts would get the job done.

Stubs cut around the pile of assorted nuts and headed his way. He stopped when he was half way there and a look of disbelief swept across his face. He turned and looked at Pete for instructions but discovered he was already cutting across Seed Man's yard, heading for the street.

Stubs looked back at Roscoe, paused for a moment, then ran after Pete.

Even though it was not part of Roscoe's plan, Manny, the giant, overweight squirrel decided he'd better come over just in case there was a problem. He'd slipped behind Roscoe long enough to be seen by Pete and Stubs but before Roscoe could turn around and discover what frightened them, he'd crept into the shadows.

Roscoe, of course, thought he was the one who caused them to run in fear.

"Come back and fight," he hollered to the retreating group. "Your not afraid of little old me are you?" He raised his paws in the air and did a little dance with his feet.

"We did it," he yelled out loud. "We took on Pete and his buddies and showed them what happens when you push someone too far."

Marvin and Jules came up beside him and joined in the celebration.

Roscoe could see Yardley dragging a large sack behind him and picking acorns off the ground.

Homer and two of his helpers climbed the tree, shoved the trap door back in place and made sure it was locked securely.

Roscoe was worn out but happy. He'd done some things in the past that had been rewarding but nothing like this. It had been a good night.

"What do you say we celebrate with a midnight snack?" Marvin gave a quick glance at the feeder to make sure there were enough seeds for all of them.

"Works for me," Jules answered.

"I'd love to but I promised Yardley I'd help gather up his acorns, then I think I'll turn in, I'm beat."

Marvin shrugged and said, "Whatever," then he and Jules cut through the tall grass at the edge of Seed Man's yard on their way to the feeder.

Roscoe called out, "Thanks guys, I couldn't have done it without you."

He smiled as he walked over to help Yardley gather his collection of nuts. When they finished he was looking forward to getting a good night sleep in his own nest.

He remembered reading somewhere that you can break a single string but if you weave several of them together their strength increases. As he thought about the friends who'd put themselves in danger by helping him with the *O'Malley Problem* he knew the saying was true.

CHAPTER 11

The Seed Maker

"Now tell me about your offer again Mr. Leo." Edgar, Chairman of the Committee for the Protection of Neighborhood Resources leaned forward in his chair. Across from him his guest with the sharply pointed face and big ears smiled; he knew from the sound in Edgar's voice he had him.

It had been two weeks since Seed Man and his wife Sweetheart had gone on vacation. And it had been the same length of time the feeder had been out of seeds. Seed Man usually checks the feeder tubes and makes sure their full before he leaves, but this time, he forgot or there was also the possibility that Sweetheart had emptied them without his knowing it. She was determined to get the squirrels out of her yard.

That's when Edgar's guest showed up. As the Community entered its third week without seeds he'd walked into the Clearing in front of the Committee meeting room pulling an odd looking cart. He announced to those present he was a professional seed maker and had come to help them through the crises they faced.

The guest cleared his throat and spoke in a high pitched, wheezy voice. "I will produce within six days more seeds than you're Community can eat or I'll walk away and you owe me nothing. And please Edgar, call me Leo."

Edgar hummed and pulled at the whiskers on his chin. He felt he should ask some important questions about the details of the arrangement but he couldn't think of any. So he hummed, hoping Lou would think he was considering other options.

"I see what's going on here Edgar," Leo smiled and poked Edgar with his elbow. "You're dragging your feet on this deal thinking you'll wait me out and I'll come down in my price." Leo gave Edgar a look of admiration for his negotiating skills. "I must say, and this shouldn't leave the room, if I was in your position I'd do exactly the same thing." Leo nodded his head knowingly.

Edgar hadn't followed everything he said but assumed from the look on his face he'd paid him a compliment. He started to say thank you but before he could Leo continued. "Just think about it. I stroll into your Community and promise to produce all the seeds you can eat. You have no idea who I am. Why should you trust me? Why should you put any faith in what I'm saying?"

Edgar tried to clear his throat but found it was dry. "That's not," is as far as he got.

Leo picked up the leather briefcase he'd carried into the meeting room. "I'll tell you why. Inside this brief case are the testimonials of those who doubted me at first and are now my most satisfied customers." He started to open the briefcase but Edgar stopped him.

"That won't be necessary Leo." I'm not really cut out for this kind of thing, Edgar thought, going over details and haggling about prices is just not me. "It's ah, just that, let's see, how shall I say it? The ah, cost for your services hasn't been mentioned." Edgar felt bad having to be the one to raise the issue of cost. He remembered hearing someone say, if you have to ask how much something costs you probably can't afford it.

"You know Edgar, a very wise person once said, and this is a very rough quote, if you have to ask how much something costs you probably can't afford it." Leo looked at Edgar and smiled. "But I understand the position your in. Most Chairman can make this kind of decision on their own but I have found the weaker ones usually have to get permission from their Committee." He raised one eye brow, asking with the gesture, "Which type of Chairman are you?"

"Oh no, no, its not that, its just, ah, you haven't actually said what you'll charge and I…" Edgar opened his paws indicating he knew his guest would understand.

Leo rummaged through his briefcase for a moment until he removed two sheets of paper covered with very small print. "It's all right here. Take your time reading it, I'm in no hurry." He handed the papers to Edgar and walked to the small window over the wooden bench.

"I knew you'd understand," Edgar started to say more but was interrupted again when Leo came back and pulled the papers from his hand before he could read the first line.

"However, it is getting late and I have an appointment with another Community who said they absolutely had to have my services, no questions asked. I was holding them off, hoping we could work something out. But…" He pushed the papers back into his briefcase.

The Squirrel Chronicles: Book One

"Could you possibly summarize the terms of the contract? Just hit the important parts?" Edgar hated to miss this chance to help the Community. He was concerned he'd loose out to the other group but he needed some idea of the cost in case someone on the Committee asked.

"Certainly Edgar, its no problem at all." He cleared his throat and spoke in a monotone. "The party of the first part, so on and so forth shall purchase the services of the party of the second part, so on and so forth who will provide all services attached hereto." He looked at Edgar who nodded he was with him so far. "At absolutely no cost to the Community," he added as he put both paws on the table and looked straight into the Edgar's eyes.

Edgar locked in on the last part, the part about his services not costing the Community anything. He told himself he'd be a fool to turn down an opportunity like this. He knew if he didn't act quickly the other Community Leo had mentioned would step in and snatch him away.

"Sign us up!" Edgar stood and walked toward Leo to touch paws on the deal.

"Don't you want to hear about the rest? The other conditions?" Leo acted surprised that Edgar was so eager to sign.

"Boilerplate. I'm sure it's nothing but boilerplate." Edgar was pleased. He'd worked out the very best deal he could for the Community who, he was sure, would be thanking him continuously and possibly even offering him the position of Committee Chairman for life because of his bold, decisive action in a time of crises.

He looked at Leo and asked, "Where do I sign?"

Leo produced the documents and Edgar signed both copies,

keeping one for himself and handing the other one back to Leo. With the paperwork out of the way he asked, "How soon before the seeds start flowing?"

"Well Edgar." Edgar flinched, something had changed in Leo's voice. The soft, friendly, open quality he'd heard moments before had turned cold, almost metallic. "Everything starts the moment you turn the keys of the Committee meeting room over to me." Leo smiled and held out his hand.

"Keys?" Edgar tried to remember if Leo had said anything about keys. "To the meeting room?" The air around him had suddenly grown warm and he had to steady himself by holding on to the back of a chair or he was sure he'd fall down.

"Well of course the keys Edgar." From Edgar's position, holding on to the chair and looking up, Leo suddenly appeared taller. "Don't you remember Subparagraph B in Section 6?"

"Subparagraph B?" Edgar had only been able to read the first two lines on the first page before Leo had yanked the papers away from him. He hadn't even made it through the introduction.

"Let me read it for you then." He took the signed papers from Edgar's paw and flipped to the second page. "Ah, here we are," he paused, shifting into a different voice that sounded to Edgar like an elevator operator calling out floor numbers as they plummeted out of control to the basement.

"The signer, that's you Edgar, shall turn over the administration of the Community to an appointed representative of Seedmaker, Inc., that's me, for the duration." He turned the page so Edgar could see and pointed to the line he'd just read.

Edgar looked but couldn't see anything because of the tears welling up in his eyes. "Duration?" His mind was spinning as it dawned on him it might have been better to have had someone else read the fine print before signing the papers. "Just how long would you say, from your experience that is, is a duration?

"Edgar," Leo put an arm around his shoulder and walked him toward the door, "that's the first good question you've asked since I walked into the room."

Leo smiled as he hustled Edgar outside then stepped back in and closed the door. The first thing he'd do was remove Edgar's things from his desk and replace them with things of his own.

What started out as a few Community members standing around the Clearing turned into a crowd with latecomers pushing for a place to stand as they watched Leo unpack his cart. The cart was painted deep blue and on two sides, *Leo the Seed Maker*, was printed in bright orange letters. He placed pinwheels on two of the corners of the cart and removed several rolls of colored material, spreading them on the ground, making a blanket of yellow and crimson. He placed a drum on top of the material and smoke began to come from somewhere inside the cart.

As he worked, Leo seemed unaware of the crowd watching him. When everything was ready he sat on the blanket and picked up the drum. He beat it slowly at first and sang a tune no one recognized. As the cadence of the drum beat picked up he sang louder until all at once, with a final bang of the drum and a yelp from him, the music stopped and he looked up.

The crowd hesitated for a moment and then followed his gaze into the tree branches overhead and were shocked when two bags of seeds fell to the ground. They landed with a thud on either side of him and broke open, spilling the contents onto the blankets.

The crowd rushed forward to help themselves; because of the

draught of seeds the usual practice of being polite and taking turns had been replaced with a first come first served attitude. Leo stood and held out his paws, making a pushing gestures, shooing them away.

"My friends, if I could have your attention for a moment." He waited for them to quiet down. "I'm Leo your new Chairman of the Committee for the Protection of Neighborhood Resources." He paused as those in the crowd whispered to each other if the stranger hadn't been mistaken, wasn't Edgar their Chairman.

Leo ignored their comments and continued. "At this time I would like introduce my administrative assistants Noland and Roland." He held out his arm and gestured for them to come forward. As they moved to their places on either side of him members of the Community asked each other if anyone had ever seen the two administrative assistants before.

No one had.

"You are probably wondering why I, your new Chairman, would need two assistants." Leo smiled and scanned the crowd. He saw several nodding their heads yes, that's exactly what they were wondering. Someone in back made the comment that, "Edgar hadn't needed an assistant, let alone two."

Leo pretended he didn't hear him. "I have two assistants because," he pointed to the bags on either side of him, "I have two bags of seeds." He raised his eyebrows asking if they followed what he'd said so far. Blank looks were the only response he got.

"Noland is responsible for the bag on my left and Roland the one on the right." He gestured for the two assistants to take their place next to the bags. When they were in position Leo continued. "My assistants will help in the distribution of the seeds to make sure all of you have an equal amount to take back to your nests."

Those in the crowd nodded they understood that part and were relieved they weren't going to have to fight with their neighbor for their share.

Leo walked to his cart, opened a door on the side and produced a bundle of lime green sacks. "To insure that everyone gets their fair share, my assistants, will put the seeds into these colorful sacks, sized to hold exactly one days worth of seeds." Leo handed an equal number of sacks to his assistants.

"That's a great idea," someone in the crowd said. Another added that was going to make it a lot easier to carry the seeds back to our nests.

"The seeds are free as agreed upon in the contract I signed with your former Chairman Edgar." Leo smiled and stepped back. Some in the crowd took that to mean it was okay to come forward and get their seeds. They took a first step but stopped when Leo started speaking again.

"However, while the seeds are free, the sacks the seeds come in are not cheap. So, we will require each of you to bring some possession from your nest and trade it for your bag of seeds." He smiled and pointed to two large sacks where they were to put the things they brought to pay for their seeds.

It had been two weeks since some members of the Community had eaten their last seed. A few of them had violated the Community rule about keeping seeds in their nests so they hadn't been out of food the whole time. Some had stooped to eating green acorns or hazelnuts and even walnuts that had fallen to the ground and started to rot. Others out of desperation to keep their families from starving had begun digging up their winter supply of nuts. "What good does it do," some had reasoned, "if there's a supply of food this winter and you're not around to eat it?"

They looked at the delicious seeds on the ground around the sacks glistening in the sunlight. They closed their eyes and imagined the taste and felt the crunch as they bit into them. They could feel the fiber split between their teeth and taste the small glob of juice released from inside the seed as it trickled down their throat. They had things in their nest they wanted to get rid of anyway, things they would be happy to give up for a bag of seeds.

One by one they left the Clearing and headed to their nests.

Leo rubbed his paws together and smiled. "Boys," he said to his assistants, "don't expect too much the first few days but by day three, they'll start bringing in the good stuff." He patted his assistants on the back, urged them to be patient, then walked the short distance from the Clearing to the meeting room.

It had been a terrible night for Roscoe. First he had trouble going to sleep because someone in the Community kept banging on a drum and singing at the top of his lungs half the night. Then, around midnight a storm rolled in and even though it was now daybreak, rain was still falling. He decided there wasn't a chance he could go back to sleep so he stretched and started down the tree thinking that getting out this early would give him a head start finding something to eat.

When he was half the way to the ground he saw someone standing at the base of his tree. Whoever it was looked like he'd been standing there for some time and was soaked clear through.

As he got closer he was surprised to discover it was Edgar. His fur was matted from the rain and he was staring straight ahead with bloodshot eyes. His teeth were chattering and he was swinging his arms in small circles to try to generate some heat.

Roscoe approached him slowly hoping to take away the element of surprise. "Edgar? What's going on?"

Edgar turned toward him and Roscoe was surprised by the vacant look in his eyes. "R-R-Roscoe? Is th-th-that you?"

"Come up to my nest Edgar, we need to get you out of the rain." Roscoe took his arm and started to move him toward the base of his tree.

"Oh R-Roscoe, wh-when you hear wh-what I've done, you ma-may change your m-mind." Edgar sighed deeply and shook his head. "I wouldn't b-blame you if you d-did."

"What could you possibly have done that…"

"I have sold out the Community Roscoe," Edgar interrupted him. Talking seemed to help; he was beginning to warm up. "I have tr-traded the trust of the members of my beloved Community for a b-bowl of porridge. I have turned my back on all those who have fa-faithfully supported me over the years. I have traded all that I hold dear for personal gain."

Roscoe thought he saw a tear start down Edgar's cheek but it was impossible to tell since he was so wet.

"Now Edgar, if you'd come up and dry off I think you'll feel a lot better." Roscoe attempted to move him towards the tree again, he was beginning to feel uncomfortable standing in the rain.

"You'd do that for me Roscoe? You'd we-welcome a Community turncoat into your home? You would offer an outcast sh-shelter from the raging s-storm?" Edgar shivered and allowed Roscoe to lead him to his nest. When they got there Roscoe found a warm, dry place in a corner and encouraged him to lie down. He fell asleep immediately but tossed and turned, mumbling about a seeds falling from the sky, Section B and someone named Leo. None of it made sense to Roscoe.

After an hour of fitful sleep Edgar woke up and spent a few moments trying to figure out where he was. Finally he saw Roscoe and remembered the chain of events that had brought him to Roscoe's nest and he started to weep again. Between sobs he talked about Leo and his ability to produce seeds from thin air and the paper work he'd signed but never had a chance to read. He talked about Roland and Noland, Leo's administrative assistants, and the seeds that dropped from the sky being free but the sacks they put them in costing a valuable possession from each member of the Community. He ended up by repeating several times there being no fool like an old fool.

When he was finished he sat back, exhausted from talking and the effects of being out in the rain all night, he fought to stay awake.

"Stay here Edgar," Roscoe told him, "Let me do some looking around."

He might as well have saved his breath, Edgar had lost the battle to fatigue and fallen asleep leaning against the side of the nest.

Roscoe knew the next "seed making event" wouldn't be for a few more hours but decided to find a spot where he could watch what was going on without being seen. He picked a place directly over Edgar's nest which, he guessed, Leo had also claimed.

There was no sign of Edgar's wife Edna.

From his position above the Clearing he had a clear view of the area in front of the meeting room and the branches directly above it.

He settled in and wished he'd brought something along to eat. He was afraid this was going to be a waste of time. There was the possibility Leo was on the up and up although the idea of producing seeds out of thin air was a little hard for him to picture. If it could be done he was sure someone would have figured it out how to do it long before Leo had.

He was thinking about that, his hunger and what he would say if someone saw him when something caught his eye. At first he thought he was mistaken but as he sat quietly in the fork of the tree he saw it again. It was the practiced movement of two squirrels he didn't recognize, creeping along the branches directly over the Clearing. He realized the thing that made them so hard to see were the camouflage outfits they wore. He was sure they would be invisible to anyone on the ground looking up.

He watched as they each pushed a bag of seeds in front of them. They nudged the bags into position, then sat down and waited. They said nothing to each other even though they were only a few feet apart. It was obvious to Roscoe this was not the first time they'd performed this maneuver.

He watched Leo step dramatically out of the meeting room, spread the colorful material on the ground and put the pinwheels on his cart. He saw him flip the switch that started the smoke machine. He opened the door on the front, removed the drum from inside and began slowly pounding on it, blending the sound of the drum with his voice.

When Leo was almost finished Roscoe watched the two camouflaged squirrels scoot forward and begin to lean against the bags. They waited until the heard the final beat of the drum and Leo's yelp, waited a second, then pushed the bags forward sending them hurtling to the ground. The crowd gathered below let out a cheer when they saw the bags fall and immediately lined up in front of Roland and Noland who'd removed their camouflaged uniforms and scampered down the tree as the bags fell.

Community members walked past the two administrative assistants, putting their possessions in the cloth bag they were holding and picking up their bag of seeds.

Roscoe had seen enough and a plan began to form in his mind as he made his way back to his nest. He stopped someone on his way to the Clearing carrying a rusty bottle cap he was going to trade for a bag of seeds. Roscoe asked him to tell Marvin and Jules to meet him at his place and make it snappy.

While they sat together in his nest, Roscoe explained what he had in mind and his two friends listened quietly. They asked a few questions like where they were going to get the rope he'd mentioned and who was going to distract the guards while they carried out their part of the plan but mostly they listened.

Several times during their meeting Edgar cried out in his sleep. He begged forgiveness from someone he thought was going to tie him up and throw him out of his nest. He called out Edna's name several times and said he was sorry for disappointing her. He argued about which were the tastiest seeds with someone named Norten who Roscoe had never heard of. Finally, just before he turned over on his side and went back to sleep, he mentioned Penny Sue's name and began to weep.

Then he grew quiet.

At the mention of Penny Sue's name, Roscoe, Marvin and Jules looked at each other and said, "Of course." Penny Sue is Edgar's very attractive granddaughter and the cause of a number of odd experiences involving Roscoe and the feeder.

Roscoe said he'd talk to her and that Marvin and Jules should look for the rope they would need. They agreed to meet back at Roscoe's nest the next morning.

When they got back together Roscoe went over the plan with

them explaining a few late breaking developments. When he was finished he looked at them. "Guys, there's no room for error on this one." They nodded they understood, joined paws in the center of the circle, said, "Seeds," and headed to their assigned tasks.

Roscoe went directly to the place in the trees he'd been the day before. Leo's workers hadn't arrived yet. He looked down and saw Penny Sue at the edge of the Clearing watching closely for a sign that would tell her it was time to go to work.

He watched the camouflaged squirrels show up and push the seed bags in position. He heard one say to the other that today the members of the Community should be digging into their good stuff in exchange for their seeds. Then they settled back and waited for the Leo Show to begin.

Roscoe gave a quick nod of his head and Penny Sue started across the area in front of the meeting room. She walked slowly, stopping occasionally for a long, luxurious stretch. One of the guards spotted her and nudged the other one with his elbow.

They both watched, spellbound by her beauty.

She walked to the box Roscoe had placed near the seed maker's cart and tried to pick it up but it was obviously too heavy for her. "Oh my, I've got to get this heavy box to my grandfather's nest and I have no one to help me. What can I possibly do?" She spoke loud enough for the observers to hear but never looked up to see if they were listening.

They sat on the limb for a second, checked to see if Leo was around and when they saw the coast was clear, hurried down the tree to come to Penny Sue's aide.

While they were gone, Marvin and Jules rushed out and tied one end of the bag of seeds with a rope and the other end to the limb they were standing on. They poked the rope under the sacks to keep them from being seen. When their work was finished they touched paws and quietly left.

Below, Penny Sue saw the second signal from Roscoe that said everything was in place. She turned to the two squirrels struggling to lift the box off the ground. "Oh silly me. That's not even the right box, I can see that from here."

They set the box down but when they stood and started to ask what her name was she was gone. They looked at each other and wondered what that was about. When they got back up to the branch that held the seed bags they relaxed, everything was just like they'd left it.

Leo waited until it was a little later in the afternoon then normal before stepping out of the Committee meeting room. He wanted to make sure they understood he was in charge now and would be the one to decide when they would eat and how much. The crowd that had formed grew quiet as he walked to his cart and began arranging things for his afternoon performance. He started tapping slowly on the drum and singing a song the crowd knew by heart. They were anxious to get their seeds and could hardly wait until he banged on the drum and yelped.

Everyone knew what came next. That's why they'd come with their best possessions, to get their daily ration of seeds. On the limbs above them the two squirrels pushed on the seed bags and smiled as they watched them slip over the limb.

But, instead of falling to the ground as they normally did, they snapped to a stop as the rope that had been tied around their tops by Marvin and Jules became taut and hung just above Leo's head.

The eyes of those in the crowd shifted from the bags to Leo who was as surprised by what happened as they were. Before anyone could react several members of the Community wearing

The Squirrel Chronicles: Book One

masks and stocking caps, darted across the Clearing and grabbed the end of the material Leo had spread on the ground. They raced through the crowd that parted for them even though Leo shouted to, "Stop those thieves."

A loud whistling sound pierced the air as Marvin and Jules let the air out of one of the tires on his cart.

Leo spun around and threw his drum at them as they ran behind the tree that housed the Committee meeting room. As they leaped out of sight the door to the meeting room flew open and Edgar stepped onto the small platform at the top of the stairs, pointed to the path that lead away from the Clearing and said as forcefully as he could, "Go!"

Those watching weren't aware of how nervous he was about returning to the Community; he almost forgot the one word he was supposed to say but Roscoe had moved in behind him and whispered it to him while he stood on the platform.

Leo turned toward Edgar. His face was red with anger and his arms were thrust down at his side. He shifted his gaze to the crowd and said, "You're going to have to make a choice today my friends." Leo flashed his brightest smile, all signs of anger were gone replaced by a look of supreme confidence.

"Will it be me, who will keep this Community in seeds or that weak, simple minded ignoramus standing on the meeting room steps?" He pointed to Edgar.

Those in the crowd whispered to each other for a moment then looked at Leo and shook their heads. Finally someone spoke up and said, "We're sticking with Edgar."

Leo couldn't believe it. "But he betrayed you. He made a deal with me that would have robbed you of your possessions and given him great wealth. Is that what your looking for in a leader?"

An older member, encouraged by those around her, stepped forward and said what they all were thinking. "Oh we know he's not the tastiest seed in the feeder tube but he means well."

They were shocked when a bolder looking Edgar stepped off the platform and repeated it was time for Leo to go. Only this time he added, "Now!"

Leo looked up in time to see Roland and Noland running up the path away from the Clearing.

Leo stood erect and hollered, "A curse on your Community. May your seeds become dry and tasteless…" He was almost finished when one of the younger members of the Community dashed into the Clearing and announced breathlessly, "He's back."

Edgar stepped forward and asked who was back but before he could finish the crowd yelled, "Seed Man. He's back." Those in the crowd hugged each other and applauded so loudly they could barely hear the young messenger say, "He was putting seeds in the feeder when I left. He should be finished about now."

Soon the crowd was gone and only Edgar and Leo were left facing each other. Leo started to say something clever and abusive but stopped, he knew it wouldn't do any good because Edgar wouldn't get it.

Instead, he grabbed the handles of his cart and began pushing it away from the meeting room. It made a squishy sound as the flat side of the tire slid across the ground. "Roland?" Leo called. "Noland? I could use a little help here."

He didn't get an answer.

Roscoe was surprised when he heard Marvin clear his throat to get his attention, he thought everyone had gone to Seed Man's yard. He looked at Marvin who raised his eyebrows, directing Roscoe's attention to the two bags of seeds hanging from the tree limb above their heads. In the excitement of the showdown with Leo and the announcement that Seed Man was back, everyone had forgotten they were there. Marvin looked at Roscoe and smiled.

"Two squirrels. Two bags of seeds. No waiting. You don't have to be as smart as Sparky to figure this one out." He put an arm around Roscoe's shoulder. "It's your dream come true buddy. Your own bag of seeds in your nest. You'll never have to go out on cold mornings or traipse through puddles of water again. If you get the urge for a late night snack you can just reach over and grab a handful."

He leaned close to Roscoe and whispered. "No one will ever know." He waited a moment before he asked, "What do you say?"

It was while Roscoe was looking at the bags overhead that it hit him. It wasn't having the seeds that was important to him but thinking about having them was. He knew he'd eventually get tired of having all the seeds he wanted but he also knew he'd never get tired of working out plans to get them.

"What do you say we break them open and have a party for everyone in the Community?" Roscoe looked at Marvin.

"Is that your final answer?" Marvin asked.

"Absolutely. Which one do you want to open first?"

CHAPTER 12

Hostage Situation

Roscoe sat by the rose bush at the edge of the yard and watched Seed Man come around the corner of the garage with a bag of seeds. He'd seen him standing at the big picture window at the back of his house drinking a cup of coffee when he noticed the feeder tubes were empty.

There should be more ceremony to this, Roscoe found himself thinking. "There should be trumpets playing when he crosses the yard with two of his neighbors walking in front of him; one to pull back the top of the feeder tube while the other one hands him the scoop. And, they should be wearing robes or at least suites instead of the shorts and tank tops they have on.

Roscoe sighed.

Ceremony or not he wished he'd get on with it because he was getting hungrier by the minute.

Marvin came from behind him and tugged at his elbow. "Rosc, they, ah, need you in the Committee meeting room."

"In a minute Marvin, Seed Man's about finished and I need something to eat, I'm starving." Roscoe kept his eye on Seed Man while he answered.

"Actually, I don't think they have that much time left." Roscoe couldn't see it but Marvin had a worried look on his face. He tugged on Roscoe's elbow again, hoping he could at least get him moving toward the Clearing.

"What are you talking about? We've got all morning Marvin. Just tell whoever they are I'll get some seeds, take a short nap and try to get there by no later than noon." Roscoe smiled, this was going to be a good day, he could feel it.

"That's not going to work Rosc, at least not today. When I left they said they wanted to see you pronto or else." Marvin took a step away thinking that might encourage him to follow.

"What could possibly be so urgent that I have to be there immediately?" There was a touch of anger in his voice. He knew how the Committee to Protect Neighborhood Resources worked, whoever came up with the expression, hurry up and wait, had to be thinking of them. They could argue for hours about whether the word acorn had one n or two and refuse to send someone over to the library to get the correct answer.

"I was told I couldn't say anything about it. They just said, 'Get Roscy over here immediately if youse wants to see Edgar and de members of youse Committee again.'" Marvin wondered if he'd said too much.

"What?" Roscoe turned toward Marvin when he recognized the word, youse. "Why didn't you say so?" He took off in a sprint down the path that leads to the meeting room.

When he got to the base of Edgar's tree, he didn't slow down. He pushed open the door, stepped inside the meeting room and started to ask what Marvin meant but stopped when he saw

Edgar sitting behind his desk, tied to his chair. There were tears in his eyes and fear was written across his face. A rag had been tied around his mouth so it would have been impossible for him to have answered if Roscoe had asked.

"Edgar, what's going on?" Roscoe had trouble believing what he was seeing.

Edgar gave a quick nod and Roscoe followed his direction. Around the walls of the room the other members of the Committee were in the same condition as he was, bound and gagged.

The whole scene didn't make sense to Roscoe until he heard the voice that cast fear in the heart of every decent squirrel in every peace loving Community. "Well, well, if it aint my old friend Roscoy. Youse managed to show up just in time to save youse little buddies here, if youse knows what I'm getting to. A minute too early, a minute too late…" his voice trailed off and left it up to Roscoe to figure out what might have happened if he hadn't arrived when he did.

It was none other than Pete O'Malley, the ultimate bully and Roscoe's nemesis since their first day of Seed School together. The last time he'd seen Pete, he and his friends were falling out of his nest, being sprayed by the sprinkler and having hundreds of nuts dropped on them. Roscoe had hoped that would be the last time they'd come around.

Someone grabbed him from behind, forced his arms behind his back and roughly tied his paws together. "So, we meets again, eh Roscy?" Roscoe recognized the gravelly voice of Stubs, Pete's bodyguard and strong-arm man.

"Easy Stubbs," Pete's voice seldom rose above a whisper. He stood with his back to Roscoe, looking at a picture E. Paul, Edgar's son, had drawn. It was titled, *The Community*, and even though it was in an abstract form, it conveyed the feeling of closeness a Community can develop.

Pete turned his head a little to study the picture from a different angle then he reached up, took it off the wall and tossed it carelessly into the wastebasket by Edgar's desk.

Edgar whimpered.

"Turn the others loose," Pete whispered. He slowly swung his arm around the room as if warning each member of the Committee to watch their step. He ended up pointing at Roscoe, "But not him."

Stubb's and two of his friends removed the cords that held the others in their chairs. As they were freed they walked past Roscoe on their way out they looked at the floor refusing to make eye contact with him. They didn't know what Pete had planned for him but they were sure of one thing, it would involve a great deal of pain. For all they knew this could be the last time they would see Roscoe.

Finally, they released Edgar. "Mr. O'Malley. I must object in the strongest terms. As Chairman of the Committee for…" That was as far as he got. Stubb's stepped in front of him and gave him a look. "One more peeps out of youse and youse'll be eating ground up seeds through a straw for de next month."

"Er, that is, on the other paw…" Edgar gave a weak smile Roscoes way. He hesitated wondering if Pete would be mad if he pulled E. Pauls picture from the wastebasket. He shrugged, decided not to press the point and hurried out of the room.

Stubbs, Pete and Roscoe were the only ones left, Pete's two friends had stepped outside to keep anyone from coming to Roscoe's aide. Stubbs took a position behind Roscoe. Pete continued looking out of the small window and chuckled quietly as he watched Community members gather in little groups. He assumed they were talking about what might be happening to Roscoe.

"I bet youse thought youse'd never see us again after youse little, 'surprise,' the last time we was in youse neighborhood." Roscoe had to strain to hear what Pete said. He started to take a step closer but Stubbs yanked on the cord around his paws and pulled him back.

"But," Pete shrugged his shoulders, "word gets around, youse know what I'm saying? The next thing youse knows someone over here says somethun to someone over there about the little stunt you pulled…" his voice trailed off and he stood quietly for a moment. "Then what happens to me and Stubbs? Huh? What happens to us when we's got no place to lay our heads at night because everyone knows youse stood up to us and gets away with it. So they decides they can do it to? It's kind of like them domino things youse push over, the first one hits another and the next thing youse knows, bingo, bango, there all over the floor of youse nest. Youse familiar with what I'm talking about here Roscy?"

Roscoe wasn't sure if he was supposed to answer or not. Pete wasn't actually looking at him when he asked the question.

Pete put his paws behind his back and sighed, "So we's gots to show them what happens when an individual such as youseself tries to make a statement like youse already done."

"Pete, you don't understand. My nest is old, the bottom gave way. It was a complete surprise to me when Seed Man's sprinkler came on. I have no idea where the nuts came from. You can't think I planned any of that." Roscoe used his most sincere voice.

"Stubbs," Pete whispered.

Stubbs stepped forward and placed the drawing Roscoe and

Homer had made showing the hinges on either side of his nest and the rope that could be pulled from the ground to make it open. Then he dropped Yardley's nut location guide on top of the drawing. "We had a little talk with youse pals Marvin and Jules about the sprinkler thing." There was a hint of laughter in his voice.

"I'm sure if they said anything you had to force it out of them." Roscoe was shaking with emotion at the thought of his friends enduring hours of torture because of him and finally, unable to take the pain any longer, telling what they knew in a moment of exhaustion before they passed out. "You must have done something terrible to them to make them talk."

"Not really. We called them in, asked about the sprinklers and they fell apart like a cheap bird feeder." This time there was no hint of laughter, it was an outright howl.

Even Pete managed a brief smile; which for him was a major show of emotion.

"So, what's next?" Roscoe tried to sound brave but underneath the bravado he was afraid. He'd seen these two in action before and didn't know what to expect other than It wasn't going to be pleasant.

"We's got no place to goes Roscy and we's in no hurry to get there. Youse planned for us, so, we plans for youse…everything works out. See what I'm saying here?" Pete hadn't moved from his position by the window. Even though the tone of his voice was sinister nothing in his body language would suggest he was doing anything other than looking out the window.

Roscoe figured the longer they took deciding what to do the better it was for him.

Outside, at a spot some distance from the meeting room, Edgar stood with the rest of the members of the Committee.

"Gentlemen, if it comes down to it, loosing Roscoe is a small price to pay for our freedom. At least now, Pete and Stubbs will get even with him and leave us alone." He paced back and forth as he talked, his paws were clasped tightly behind his back.

"You can't mean that Edgar," Darin, a member of the Committee spoke up. "Roscoe has come to the aide of our Community so many times I've lost count not to mention saving your own granddaughter, twice if I'm not mistaken. Besides, how do you know, once Roscoe is out of the way, they won't decide to come and stay in your nest? And that goes for the rest of you." He looked each member of the Committee in the eye, disappointed they weren't willing to stand up for Roscoe when he needed them. As he did they either looked at the ground or at something in the distance.

"That's an excellent point Darin, an excellent point." Edgar stopped pacing. "Anybody got an idea about how to spring Roscoe loose from a room with two mean and unprincipled ruffians who are holed up in a tree surrounded by guards?"

The Committee remained silent.

"Is there any way we come down from inside the tree? That way we'd take the guards out of the picture," one of them finally asked breaking the silence.

"From the bottom of my nest on down to the Committee room ceiling it's solid oak." Edgar spoke from experience, he'd helped hollow out the space for the meeting room.

"What if we get all the members of the Community together and overpower the guards? There's more of us than there is of them."

"The noise would tip off those inside and who knows what they'd do to Roscoe if they panicked?" Edgar spoke for the group.

"How about we throw nuts at the guards?"

"Or, catch them while they're sleeping?"

"We could sneak through the trees and drop a net on them, you know, take them by surprise."

Everyone had an idea and before long several small groups formed, each arguing over the merit of their plan and trying to explain why it would succeed where the others wouldn't.

"Please. Please. This isn't going anywhere. Why don't we all go to our nests, get something to eat and come back with some fresh ideas." Edgar looked exhausted. He knew they couldn't take all day on this, Roscoe's life was hanging by a thread. At the same time, no one had come up with even the faintest glimmer of an idea that might work.

"Hold on a minute," Darin had started to walk away but stopped when a thought popped into his head. "If we have to eat, so do they."

Edgar turned and gave Darin a look that said, "Aren't you stating the obvious? We all have to eat." He shook his head wondering how he got hooked up with such an incompetent group.

"But," someone in the crowd saw where Darin's idea was headed and spoke up. "We can go to the feeder and they can't."

Those around the last speaker patted him on the shoulder, congratulating him on having the courage to say what was on his mind.

"Could we move off this idea of eating? All they have to do is walk out of the meeting room or send someone for seeds…" Suddenly Edgar saw what Darin was talking about. If the guards could somehow be drawn away from their posts those inside the room would never know and that increased the chances of getting Roscoe away safely.

"But, what if they don't go out for seeds? What if they planned for others to bring food to them? What if they send out for food and have it delivered?" Edgar stopped because he knew the average squirrel could only handle two what ifs at a time. When he reached the third if, he could tell from the look on their faces he'd gone one if, too far.

They were silent for a moment and then it was as if the same idea hit them at the same time. There was someone in their Community capable of the upper level thinking required to consider three what ifs at once. "Sparky," they said.

Edgar led the group to Sparky's laboratory. Since he was Chairman of the Committee and the one who would have come up with the idea that the captors had to eat sometime if Darin hadn't beat him to it, he crossed the open space in front of the laboratory.

Lights from high in the trees flashed on and off and a whistle blew. A mechanical voice penetrated the clamor, "Step away and identify."

Edgar called in his loudest voice, "Sparky, we have no time for this foolishness." He stepped up to the door thinking he'd push it open and walk into the lab. He was about to say his friend Roscoe was in trouble but never got it out because he was hit with a bucket of water dropped from someplace above the entrance.

"Sparky," he sputtered.

"Step away and identify," the mechanical voice repeated.

"Sparky you don't understand. Your friend Ros…" Nuts began to drop from the tree above him and bounced off his head and shoulders.

He staggered from the blows, stood still for a moment then fell face down in the wet grass in front of the laboratory.

Darin stepped to one side of the door, called out his name and explained that Roscoe was in trouble.

The door to the laboratory opened and Sparky appeared. He was wearing a white lab coat with his name printed over the top of the pocket.

"What's this about Roscoe?"

Everyone tried to speak at once until Sparky asked them to stop and let Darin explain why they'd come.

Darin knew Sparky was a stickler for detail so he started at the beginning about Pete taking the members of the Committee hostage until Roscoe came. He told him about Pete letting everyone go and how he and Stubbs were keeping Roscoe tied to a chair in the meeting room. He added the last part, about how they figured they were going to get hungry at some point and that was as far as they were able to get because things had gotten too complicated for them.

Sparky tugged on his chin hairs and stared at Darin, but it was obvious he was so deep in thought he didn't see anything or anyone.

They heard the sound of glass break inside the laboratory.

Sparky blinked and said, "Come inside there's someone I want you to meet."

As they entered the lab they saw a young squirrel, sitting on a stool in the center of the room. "Uncle Sparky I didn't touch anything, honest. I was just sitting here and, okay, I saw your yoyo on the shelf and I thought since I wasn't doing anything…" He stopped when he saw there were others with him.

"Edgar, Darin, I'd like you to meet my cousin, Casey but everyone in our family calls him…"

Casey started to get up and touch paws with the visitors but somehow the end of his tail was pinned beneath one of the legs of the stool. He fell one way and the stool went the other. As he fell, he grabbed the edge of a shelf to stop his fall. Instead of supporting him it gave way and several glass jars containing items Sparky had collected for study slid off and hit the floor of the lab, breaking in pieces. The stool banged against a box and they heard something inside break.

"Oops, sorry Sparky, I was, I mean I didn't..." he tried to set the stool back up but became tangled in its legs and fell again.

"Klutz," Sparky finished what he started to say before the incident with the stool. "We call him Klutz."

Edgar and Darin stared, their mouths open in disbelief, they'd never seen anything like this.

Sparky helped his cousin to his feet and told the visitors, "I think we just found the answer to our problem."

"I'm afraid you've lost me Sparky," Edgar was the first to speak.

Darin nodded in agreement, he was as confused as Edgar.

"If one of you would get a nut cake I'll..." Sparky's voice trailed off as he went to the back of the lab.

Edgar looked at Darin and asked, "Did he say nut cake?"

Most of the Committee members had returned to the Clearing and were gathered with their friends outside the meeting room. Some decided to stop by the feeder before returning to their vigil. Occasionally they'd see Pete come to the small window look out and then step away.

They knew they didn't have much time to come up with a plan to free Roscoe. To make matters worse, Edgar and Darin, the one's they depended on for leadership in a time of crises, hadn't come back from Sparky's.

They turned when they heard someone walking down the path to the Clearing, thinking it was Edgar arriving with a plan to get Roscoe out of his dilemma. Instead they saw a stranger, carrying a sack. They watched him stop, set the sack on the ground and shake his arm, apparently tired from carrying whatever was in the sack. He bent down to pick it up, lost his balance and fell, almost landing on the package.

He wore a blue shirt with a small patch on the front that said, *"Nut Cakes To Go,"* hurriedly stitched in white thread. When he finally got to the Clearing he asked the first group he came to for directions to the meeting room. They pointed to the base of the tall tree at the edge of the Clearing. He thanked them and turned to cover the remaining ten steps to the tree. As he started to move again, he twisted in an odd way and tipped sideways causing several of those near by to grab his arm to keep him from falling again.

Someone picked his cap off the ground and placed it back on his head. He thanked them and approached the steps in front of the door to the meeting room.

"Sorry fella' no can do." One of the guards patrolling the area outside the meeting room stepped in front of him. "You can't go no farther."

"Oh, but I, I mean, I'm supposed to deliver…" He pulled off a small piece of paper clipped to the top of the sack and read, "Pete something, I can't make out the other name."

The guard could smell the warm nut cake in the sack. "Let me see what you got there." When he bent down to look at the paper, Klutz stepped closer to show him the name on it. When he did their heads collided sending the guard staggering backward. A dazed look crossed his face before he fell over backwards.

Several members of the Community figured out what had happened, rushed over to the fallen guard and dragged him away. When they got him to the Clearing one of them ran to get some rope.

Klutz blinked and looked around. He thought he'd been talking to someone but decided whoever it was must have gone.

He took another step toward the door.

"Hey, hey, hey. Youse better stop right where youse is." The other guard was making his rounds and thought he'd heard something. He'd come around to check it out and was surprised to see the small delivery squirrel with a sack under his arm.

"Take off little guy our youse gonna end up stuffed in the sack youse's carrying if youse is capable of comprehending what I'm sayen." The guard smacked a fist in his paw to emphasize he wasn't kidding.

"Oh, sure, right. I see what you're saying. I just, well this paper said," Klutz fished around in his shirt pocket, trying to find the delivery slip he placed there after talking to the first guard. He found it but it was harder to remove his paw now that he was holding on to the piece of paper. Apparently, when Sparky sewed the pocket on the shirt, he'd misjudged how much room was required to remove a paw holding a piece of paper.

"Hey, hey. What are youse…" The guard leaned forward to see what was going on and when he did, Klutz applied enough force to break the stitches of the pocket and free his paw. His fist shot out and struck the guard on the chin. He staggered for a moment and fell over, unconscious.

"Gee whiz, I'm sorry I just wanted to show you…" He held up the piece of paper in front of the fallen guard. While he spoke another group ran across the Clearing and grabbed the feet of the second guard.

Klutz straightened his shirt and tried to push the torn pocket back in place as he walked up the steps to the meeting room. His back foot caught on the top step and threw him forward into the door.

Stubbs thought he'd heard a moan from outside and decided to see what it was. It bothered him that he hadn't seen either guard pass by the window in awhile.

When he opened the meeting room door he was struck in the stomach by Klutz who was trying desperately to regain his balance. The last thing he wanted to do was have something happened to the sack with the nut cake he was supposed to deliver.

Stubbs lay on the floor in front of him gasping for breath.

"Oh my, I'm sorry, see, I tripped on the step and then you opened the door." Klutz wasn't sure what to do. He couldn't help Stubbs unless he put the nut cake down. But, didn't want to put the nut cake down because he wanted to show his uncle Sparky he could be counted on to complete a simple task like delivering a nut cake.

As he was looking for a place to put the sack he swung it around and struck Pete in the side of the head with it. Pete looked surprised and fell over backward.

"Oh, boy I'm afraid I did it that time. I'm…" Klutz looked around the room, not sure what to do, he didn't know which one to help first.

Members of the Committee rushed into the room and tied the paws and feet of Pete and Stubbs, hurried them out of the room and took them to the Clearing where they placed them next to the two guards.

"Hey Guys," Klutz called from the meeting room door, "who's supposed to sign for this nut cake?"

"Bring it with you Klutz, we're going back to my place to

celebrate." Sparky was proud of his nephew, he'd managed to bring down four of the meanest squirrels in the Neighborhood. Now, he thought to himself, with this confidence booster he may turn out to be a…

He stopped thinking when he heard a, "Woops," and a thump as Klutz fell down the stairs and landed on the ground beside him.

"Then again," Sparky shrugged, "maybe not." He helped Klutz to his feet, dusted him off and put an arm around his shoulder. As they walked together up the path to the lab Klutz tried to explain how he'd tried to deliver the nut cake but couldn't get anyone to stay around long enough to tell him who ordered it.

Sparky told him not to worry about it.

Suddenly it was quiet in the Clearing. Everyone had gone to Sparkys and taken the four kidnappers with them.

"Hello." Roscoe called from inside the empty meeting room. "I could use a little help here." He tugged at the ropes that held him to the chair.

He could hear laughter and singing coming from the direction of Sparky's lab.

He knew someone on the Committee would eventually remember him. He figured when they did Edgar would call an emergency meeting to decide who should come and untie him.

"Why am I not surprised?" he said aloud in the empty room. He tried to find a comfortable position because he knew with the Committee involved it could take awhile.

CHAPTER 13

The Society of Ben Hog

Roscoe knew he'd put off studying to become a member of *The Society of Ben Hog* way too long. *The Night of Important Questions* was less than 24 hours away and other than telling himself several times that he'd better get started, he hadn't done a thing.

It was an honor to be asked to join the Society but something was bothering him about the whole thing. Maybe it was because his buddies Marvin and Jules hadn't been asked to join with him. The three of them had talked about being members of *The Society* and going to meetings together since they were in seed school but it looked like that plan would be on hold a while longer.

He made his way over to the Community library and said hello to Webster the librarian who waved to him from the break room. He pulled the worn, leather bound volume of, *The Sphere; A Brief History*, from the shelf.

He sat down at a table, opened the book and began to read.

Ron Ostlund

The following is a true and honorable account of the finding of the Sphere as described by Lester to Montgomery, the recording secretary of the Committee for the Protection of Neighborhood Resources.

I was in the tall grass at the edge of the yard waiting for my turn at the feeder when a white sphere fell from the sky. It bounced twice and came to rest under a fern leaf next to me.

I waited to see what would happen but once it came to rest it remained motionless. I was about to take a closer look but stopped when I saw Seed Man walking around the yard waving a stick back and forth through the grass. He lifted a branch and poked under the rose bush at the corner of the house looking for something. Apparently I wasn't the only one who saw the sphere fall.

When it got too dark for him to look any longer he went inside his house. It was reported by others that several times during the evening he came to the large picture window and looked out, searching the edges of his yard for some sign of the sphere.

After a little exploratory work I discovered the sphere was easy to roll so I brought it back to the Clearing, stopped in front of the Committee meeting room and immediately notified Eugene, Chairman of the Committee. He called for Abner, the founder of our Community and someone known for his wisdom, to read the inscription on the side of the sphere. He said the first word was **Ben** but could only read the first three letters of the second word because the last two were obscured by a large gash. The letters he could read were, **Hog**. It was impossible for him to tell for sure what the remaining letters were because the gash had cut them in two. He explained they could be **KN** but that a strong argument could be made for **AN** rendering the last word Hogkn or Hogan. The final reading of the inscription on the sphere by Abner was, **Ben Hog.**

This is a faithful and true account of the finding of the sphere and the interpretation of the inscription written thereon.

The Squirrel Chronicles: Book One

It was signed by Lester and Montgomery. Abner had signed it and Eugene had written, "Our Founder," beside Abner's name because Abner would never have written it himself. Roscoe was surprised to find his grandfather Ruben's name in the list of witnesses that filled most of the last page.

He closed the book and tried to picture what it would have been like to have been there the night the Sphere fell from the sky. His thoughts were interrupted by the sound of footsteps crossing the library floor.

"Roscoe," a voice close to his ear whispered, not wanting to disturb the others in the room. It was Edgar, current Chairman of the Committee. "Outside," he said and made a gesture with his head to indicate Roscoe should follow him. "Now," he added for emphasis. Edgar smiled at the others in the library and said, "Enjoy your reading, this is of no great importance," as he hurried Roscoe toward the door.

Once outside Edgar grabbed Roscoe's arm and directed him to a place where he was sure their conversation couldn't be overheard.

"I want to talk to you for a minute about a matter of grave consequence." His voice was just above a whisper, Roscoe had to lean forward to hear him.

"*Grave* consequence? Did someone go the way of all squirrels?" Roscoe thought Edgar was joking so he decided to play along. Then he saw the serious look on his face.

"It's about the Sphere," Edgar looked around after he said it trying to determine if anyone else heard him. His tail twitched.

"Hold it Edgar, I think maybe I missed something." Roscoe was having trouble hooking up the idea of how a matter of grave consequence was related to the Sphere.

"You know already?" Edgar stepped back, astonished.

"Know what already?" Things were getting more complicated for Roscoe with each word Edgar spoke.

"That the Sphere is missing." Edgar spoke louder than he'd intended. Two Community members visiting at the edge of the Clearing stopped talking and looked his way.

"Missing? The Sphere?" It was gradually dawning on Roscoe what Edgar was talking about and why he was so upset. As Chairman of the Committee he was also the, *Highly Exalted Keeper of the Sphere* and no one holding the office had ever lost it.

"Okay. Take it easy. I'll get a group together and track it down. Whoever took it couldn't have gone far." Roscoe was all movement; his mind working as quickly as his body.

"Ah, we have a pretty good idea who took it." Edgar's shoulder's sagged, his lower lip quivered and he looked like he was about to cry. He produced a crumpled note and handed it to Roscoe.

Roscoe flattened it out and read,

> "We have youse speer so don't go around like youse is looking for it or something, Pete will get real mad and things like that."

It was signed by Stubs, Pete's personal assistant, otherwise known as his bodyguard.

There was a PS at the bottom of the page.

> "And don't think weed be so stupid as to leave de speer close by do youse?"

Beneath the PS he'd written,

> "Stubs again."

The Squirrel Chronicles: Book One

Pete O'Malley is the area bully. He hadn't just picked out the Community of Abner to terrorize, he did it to all the squirrel Communities in the area.

"Hey," he'd say with a shrug when asked, "I'm an equal opportunity bully; what can I say?" Then he and Stubs would laugh and Stubs would say, "Dat's a good one boss."

You never knew when they would show up and take over your nest so you didn't have a chance to prepare for it.

Apparently Pete had taken a fancy to the Sphere.

Edna, Edgar's wife, rushed into the area. She approached two Community members and said something. They listened then pointed in Edgar and Roscoes direction.

"Edgar dearest love," she said as she walked toward him, "we need to talk."

"Could it wait my little munchkin? I'm talking to Roscoe at the moment." He didn't want to share the nature of their conversation and alarm her. He turned back to Roscoe and rolled his eyes saying without words, this is what happens after you're joined.

"I'm sure, my sweet walnut that your conversation with, oh hello Roscoe." She nooded to Roscoe but kept her eyes on Edgar. "Is important but I think you should know that…" She stopped when Edgar put up his paw.

"Plum blossom, if you will wait a teensy moment until Roscoe and I are finished I'll be happy to help in anyway I can." Edgar smiled, hoping that would put an end to the interruption. He grew serious and added for emphasis, "It's Community business."

"But dearest acorn," her voice took on an edge, "so is this."

"My sweetest nut cake, this is most urgent." Edgar's smile was fading.

"Macadamia nut so is mine."

"Hazelnut, we're talking about, Pete O'Malley." He hated to even say the name in public. He cringed inside when he saw the couple who had directed Edna his way, look surprised and begin to whisper to each other. He knew the Community well and what he'd hoped to take care of quietly would now spread to everyone in a matter of minutes.

"Yes, my sunflower seed, that's why I came." Edna moved closer to Edgar, even on her toes the top of her head barely reached his shoulders

Edgar looked at her. "You came about Pete O'Malley? But how could you know, I mean, what made you think…"

Roscoe stepped in when he saw Edgar struggling to find the right word, he seemed unable to complete the simplest sentence. "I just learned he stole the Sphere of Ben Hog and I'm about to form a group to find it."

"Thank you for that information Roscoe," she gave Edgar a hard look. "I'm glad one of you is capable of semi-intelligent speech." She turned to go then stopped and said, "You don't need to form a group to look for him, Pete I mean. And, you don't have to have an emergency Committee meeting and waste valuable time trying to think of places where someone would hide the Sphere."

She faced Edgar. "Because I know where he is."

"You know, that is, you knew, when you came over here? Dearest brazil nut why didn't you…" Edgar was pleading for her to understand his predicament. Normally he had no trouble speaking in front of large groups but facing his wife, the top of who's head barely came to his shoulder, and hearing her say she knew the whereabouts of the Sphere had taken him by surprise.

"Ah, Edna, would you mind telling us where it is?" Roscoe

tried to use his calmest, most confident voice, hoping the panic he felt didn't show.

"I will tell you what I have been trying to tell you since I got here." She tapped a foot and put her paws on her hips. "He's taken over our nest and has that ridiculous looking sphere with him and I want to know what you're going to do about it?" She leaned closer to Edgar, and looked him straight in the eye. "So, mister big shot in the Community, I can't talk to you right now because I'm busy with matters of grave consequence. WHERE DO WE SLEEP TONIGHT? Huh? What is going to happened to the picture of our precious granddaughter Penny Sue? And my dear mother's antique seed collection…" She stood back exhausted from yelling and frightened by her knowledge of what other nests in the Community looked like when Pete left them.

Edgar stepped forward and put an arm around her shoulder. "Did he say what he wanted my little dandelion?" His voice was gentle, he patted her shoulder.

Through sobs she answered, "He said something about the Society of Ben Hog."

"Did he say he wanted to join lambkins?" Edgar hoped to coax a little more information from her before she broke down completely.

"No, sweetkins, he doesn't want to join it, he wants to run it. He wants to be the *Highly Exalted Keeper of the Sphere*." When she finished she collapsed in his arms.

"Oh, dear," was all Edgar could say as he struggled to keep his wife from falling to the ground. He looked at Roscoe and mouthed, "Do something."

Roscoe thought for a moment then took off for the Library; he needed Webster's help.

When he got there he asked for all the information he had on the *Society* and particularly what the duties of the *Highly Exalted Keeper of the Sphere* were. He learned they were mostly ceremonial, entertaining visiting Chairpersons from other Communities. He is also responsible for its care and safe keeping. A footnote Roscoe found at the bottom of the second page said, *"He will protect the Sphere from invaders regardless of the cost to his person and personal fortune."*

Roscoe reread the note making sure he had the wording right then closed the book and started to leave the library.

One of the librarians called after him, "Hey Roscoe, you dropped something."

He looked back and saw an envelope on the floor, it's original white color had aged to a soft yellow.

He said thanks, picked up the envelope and read the printing on the front. *"Open only if the Society is facing a matter of grave consequence.* That's odd, he thought, those are the exact words Edgar used.

He broke the seal, pulled out a piece of paper, unfolded it and discovered he was looking at an order of service for the, *Installation of the Highly Exalted Keeper of the Sphere."* He checked the other side of the page hoping it might have some instructions or at least provide an explanation of what was written on the front but it was blank.

He was about to throw the paper away and consider it was stuck in the book as a prank by a student who'd been studying late at night to prepare for the *Night of Important Questions.*

"What do you have there Roscoe?" Webster joined him at the side of the room and looked over his shoulder at the paper.

"Nothing I can use, unfortunately." He handed the paper to Webster and started to leave. He had more important things to do than sit around and read something written by a bored student who knows how many years ago.

"I wonder why it keeps repeating that?" Webster mumbled as he continued to scan the paper. He was about to start back through a second time when Roscoe asked, "Repeating what?"

Roscoe came back and stood next to Webster who pointed to at least three places in the program where, "Do Not Drop the Ball," had been written.

Roscoe read the note again then stared at the top of a bookshelf as he thought about what the words might mean. He blinked and said, "That's it." He took the page from Webster's paw, carefully folded it in half, folded it again and then slipped it back into the envelope.

"Thanks Webster I think you just saved all of us a lot of trouble." Roscoe patted him on the shoulder and headed out the library door.

"All I said was…" Webster didn't have a chance to finish because Roscoe was out of the library and down the steps headed for Sparky's lab.

While Roscoe was in the library Edna was finally able to support herself, although her legs were still wobbly. Edgar was leading her back to their nest so she could lie down and rest.

"Dat would be like close enough, if youse knows what I'm speaking of." Stubs stepped from behind a tree and stood between them and their nest.

"This is an outrage," Edgar left Edna leaning against the trunk of a tree and walked toward Stubs. "I will not stand for it!"

"Dat's pretty funny there Ed-garr." Stub's drug out the last part of his name as a form of ridicule. "You don't want to end up getting yourself hurt now do youse?"

"Can't you see this woman is ill?" Edgar pointed to Edna "She needs rest."

Stubs looked at Edna. "She don't look so sick to me. Not like de time she held me back in seed school. She didn't look to sick then, if youse follows what I'm saying."

Edgar had a confused look on his face. Even though he'd tried to follow carefully what Stub's said, he couldn't figure out if he was saying, "Yes, you can go up to your nest," or, "No, you'll be spending the night on the ground."

A voice, barely above a whisper, came from overhead. "Youse having a little trouble or something Stuby?"

Stub's looked up. "Naw, not really boss." He turned his attention back to Edgar and Edna. "Beat it if youse knows what's good for you'se. I'm tired of trying to reason this out wid ya."

Edna started to step forward but Edgar held her arm. "Easy lady bug, he means business. We can stay in the Committee meeting room until they leave." Edgar turned her around and began to move toward the stairs at the entrance to the meeting room.

"Dat would fall under the category of a negative idea there Eddie." It took Edgar a moment to realize Stubs was talking to him, he hadn't been called Eddie since his last year in seed school. "Pete has plans to use it dis evening when he has a few of his close friends over for a little gets together. So like, I'm takin a look at the guest list here," he held up his empty paw and studied it, "and I couldn't help noticen youse name is not on it." Stubs took a step toward them and said in a voice that had changed from playful to menacing, "Youse stayen in the room is out so scram."

"But I am Chairman of the Committee." Edgar's spoke in a high pitched whine. "I am somebody in this Community." Edgar shook Edna and said, "Isn't that true cinnamon bun?"

Edna nodded yes and would have added peach blossom if she hadn't been so tired.

"Den youse shouldn't have no trouble finding one of youse many loyal subjects to stay wid." Stubs chuckled and said he had to remember that one and tell it to Pete.

Edna and Edgar stood for a moment gathering their thoughts. Try as they might they couldn't think of anyone in the Community who would be willing to share their nest with them for the night.

"So, do you think you can do it?" Roscoe had made it past Sparky's security system and was standing next to him in his laboratory.

"Sure, no problem." Sparky scratched his head as he spoke. "I'm thinking of using an electromagnet and a small remote device that could…"

Roscoe held up his paw. "Sparky I don't want to know how it will work. The big question is, can you have it ready in time."

"I don't see why not. I'll have to get some parts and wire it up. Why don't you stop by in a few days and I'll be able to tell you exactly when you can expect it."

Roscoe shook his head. "How about rigged and operational by late this afternoon?"

Sparky blinked as his mind searched for ways to rearrange his schedule and simplify the design. "I'll have to push a few projects aside but, there's a chance I can get it done. Yea, I think so."

Roscoe was familiar with the look on Sparky's face. He knew saying anything more was useless. Sparky was already working out the details to meet the new schedule.

Roscoe let himself out and cut across the back of Seed Man's yard. He needed to get one more piece in place before what he decided to call, *Operation Save the Sphere*, could get underway.

"Hey Marvin," Roscoe called to his friend, "have you seen Sesil B?"

Sesil's name is actually Cecil but when he came back from film school he told everyone he wanted to be called Sesil and, without any explanation, added a B to the end of it.

Marvin was crossing the Clearing on his way to the library. "Someone said he's out by the dump shooting the final scene for his, *Squirrel Gangs of New York*, movie. Why, what's going on?"

"Nothing at the moment but hang on, I may need you later." Roscoe spoke over his shoulder as he continued across the Clearing.

He made his way past Edgar's nest and heard Pete tell his guests, "So he looks at his paw and says, I don't see youse name on the guest list." Roscoe heard his guests laugh politely. He heard Pete say, "Oh, I guess I should have told youse his paw was empty." Someone said, "Oh, I see," and laughed some more.

Roscoe picked up his pace and made it to the dump just in time to see four warriors trained in the martial arts drop from a tree. They lit in a circle around an actor dressed in turn of the century human clothing carrying a leather brief case.

"Sesil B., you got a minute?" Roscoe called out.

"Cut. Stop the cameras. Stop the action. Everyone relax." Sesil B. stormed from behind a tree where he and his cameraman had been filming the final fight scene in the movie. He slipped on the pair of half glasses hanging around his neck by a gold chain and hollered, "Who has the nerve to interrupt? Who would be so careless…" He looked at Roscoe and said, "Oh, it's you, I might have known." He took a few steps closer. "Is it your personal mission to destroy this movie? Are you one of those "non-violent" types who object to some of the scenes depicting the reality of the lives of squirrels in the 1900's? Is it part of your agenda to disrupt the most dramatic scene in the film?" It looked

The Squirrel Chronicles: Book One

like he could have kept on for awhile so Roscoe interrupted. "I want to talk to you about a job."

Sesil B. stared at the ground for a moment trying to move away from his anger and refocus on this new job opportunity. He reached out with his paws and formed a circle with his arms. He hummed for a moment then asked, "Media?"

"Live," Roscoe responded.

"Indoor or outdoor?" Sesil B. removed his glasses and tapped them against his cheek.

"Yet to be decided." Roscoe knew the worst thing you could do to Sesil B was limit his creative skills by narrowing his options.

"Motivation?"

"To save a Community of squirrels and rid them once and for all of an evil power while at the same time restoring to it's rightful place an object of great pride."

"Beautiful. I love it." He'd put his glasses back on and looked over the top of them. "What do you have in mind?"

Roscoe produced the sheet of paper that had fallen from *The Big Book of Important Things* he'd read in the library and handed it to him.

Sesil B glanced at the paper then locked his paws behind his back and began pacing in a large circle around Roscoe.

The actors who'd dropped from the trees when Roscoe showed up came over to ask if him if he wanted to shoot the scene over again but stopped when they saw the way he was walking. They'd seen him like this before and knew the one thing they didn't want to do was interrupt him while he was creating.

He lifted his paws and framed a square with his fingers. "I'm seeing a ceremony here, an installation service.' He gave a quick look in Roscoe's direction to make sure he was following him. "Right? Not too big but grand enough to be remembered." He continued pacing. He took his glasses off and put them back on.

"When are you thinking of staging this production?" He stopped pacing and his assistant handed him his day planner. He flipped through the pages looking for the first open date.

"Tonight." When he saw the look on Sesil B's face he added. "I realize it's short notice but we don't have the luxury of time." As an afterthought he said, "I know you're used to working with tight schedules."

Sesil B. nodded and said. "Then we haven't a moment to loose."

Roscoe hated to bring it up but felt it was better to get it out of the way at the start rather than let his plans get too far along. "You're not going to be able to have warriors drop from the tree limbs in this one Sesil B."

Sesil B. got a stunned look on his face. "But that's my signature scene. My fans expect it from me. How will they know it's a Sesil B. production if there's no…" He gave a weak smile when he saw Roscoe shake his head no. Finally he nodded and sighed, "I guess it's time I take my directing in an exciting new direction."

He looked directly at Roscoe and smiled. "I'm feeling it Roscoe." He resumed pacing and gesturing wildly with his paws. "I'm feeling the despair of the oppressed Community. The meanness of the evil intruders. The exaltation of the Community as they experience true freedom for the first time. He turned and faced Roscoe. "Oh yes, I'm definitely feeling it."

Roscoe watched Sesil B. hurry off with the actors, gesturing with his paws the rolls each of them would play in the evenings production.

Now, all Roscoe had to do was wait until dark and hope Sparky had come through for him.

Late that afternoon Sesil B knocked on the Committee meeting room door where Pete and his friends had moved when Edgar's nest had become too messy for them.

Stubs answered.

"I'm running out of daylight Mr. Stubs. Please tell your boss the ceremony will start in five minutes." Sesil B. tapped his foot as a way of emphasizing they had little time to loose.

"I think youse come to the wrong tree buddy. We got no ceremony going on in here." Stubs was puzzled by Sesil B., he'd never seen anyone quite like him. He was half his size and his glasses hung from a gold chain around his neck. The bill of his cap pointed to the back and his vest was filled with camera lenses and light meters.

"If he wishes to be installed as Highly Exalted Keeper of the Sphere he will be outside in five minutes! DO I MAKE MYSELF CLEAR?" Sesil B. was on his toes, leaning into Stub's chest. He held his position for a moment then turned and walked away from the door.

"What seems to be da problem there Stuby?" Pete heard raised voices and couldn't think of anyone foolish enough to address Stubs that way.

"Nuttin I can't handle Boss. Some little guy was talkin' about some kind of spear, that's all." Stubs closed the door and started back across the meeting room floor.

"Sphere, Stuby. How many times do I gotta tell youse? It's called a sphere." Pete left his seat at the table, walked over to the small window and looked out. "So, what'd he say about the Sphere?"

"Somethin, I don't know, hugely exhausted something. I

wasn't really payin no attention. I think he said the Speer thing needed insulation." It bothered Stubs to keep getting questions about what went on at the door, his memory of the conversation wasn't all that good.

While Pete thought about what Stubs said he watched the activity in the area in front of the meeting room. Community members arrived, some wearing colorful robes. They formed lines on either side of the steps leading up to the door of the meeting room leaving an open space between them. He saw Edgar wearing a purple robe with stars and a moon on it standing at the far end of the row. It looked to Pete like he was praying; he'd look up then gesture for the two columns of Community members to shift a few inches to one side or the other, then he would look up again.

Finally he saw him give a thumbs up sign, pick up a piece of paper and unfold it. When everything was ready, Edgar looked expectantly toward the meeting room door.

Pete heard Sesil B. say, "Action," and the door to the meeting room swung open. He looked down the two rows of Community members and saw Edgar, paper in hand, waiting at the end of the line.

Sesil B. appeared at the door. "Mr. O'Malley, IF you wish to become the Highly Exalted Keeper of the Sphere you must be installed." There was a pause and for a moment, no one moved. "NOW!" He gestured with his arm as he spoke, pointing to the door and the honor guard waiting outside. He spun around on the top step, hollered, "Roll um," and hurried to a canvas chair at the edge of the Clearing.

Pete hesitated for a moment then, caught up in the excitement of seeing Edgar in the robe of the Highly Exalted Keeper of the Sphere and the crowd of interested on lookers, fell in behind the honor guard and gestured for Stubs to follow.

The Seed School choir sang, *Lo, One Night the Sphere Appearing*, as Pete, walking between the rows of witnesses, moved toward Edgar.

Stubs walked behind him and said, "Boss dis don't look like such a good thing, youse knows what I'm sayin?"

Pete moved on, thinking how happy he was that he had taken the Sphere and all the great things he'd do when he became the Highly Exalted Keeper of it. The procession stopped and Sesil B gestured for him to continue to the end of the row and stop in front of Edgar.

When he was finally in the proper place, Edgar brought his paws together indicating the choir should stop singing. A strange silence filled the Clearing and thrilled the Community members who were seeing the installation service for the first time; it was usually performed at a secret location for members only.

Edgar spoke, reading from the paper. "Honored guests and assembled Committee and Community members, welcome to the installation service of Pete…"

"Peter," Pete whispered to Edgar.

Edgar looked up and took a step backward. He motioned for Pete to follow. He did.

"The installation of Peter O'Malley as the Highly Exalted Keeper of the Sphere of Ben Hog."

Roscoe was standing by the meeting room door and for the first time was able to look up and see if part B of his plan was in place. He smiled when he saw the gleaming white sphere hanging from a limb, twenty feet above the head of Pete O'Malley. He wasn't sure how this was going to work but as he'd said before, he didn't have to know as long as Sparky did.

He turned his attention back to Edgar.

"I will read from the ancient order of service." Edgar held up the paper for all to see and cleared his throat.

"Being the Highly Exalted Keeper of the Sphere is a sacred duty Peter. DO NOT DROP THE BALL!" His voice rose as he read the last part.

He nodded that it was Petes turn to respond. "Okay," Pete said.

Edgar looked up, then back at Pete. "DO NOT DROP THE BALL!" He looked directly at him to make sure he understood.

"Okay, okay I heard you'se de first time, all right?" Pete looked at one of the members standing to his right and shook his head. "I'm not stupid or nothing."

"Peter, repeat after me the final solemn vow of installation." Edgar continued unfazed by Pete's outburst.

"Sure, no problem," Pete shrugged, relieved the ceremony was almost over. Usually, he preferred to operate behind the scene and let Stubs do the talking.

Edgar spoke in a loud voice, "I Peter O'Malley will not."

Pete started in his usual husky, high pitched voice but spoke a little louder when he saw Edgar put a paw to his ear indicating he couldn't hear him.

"I Peter O'Malley will not."

"Drop the ball." Edgar gave him a deadly serious look.

Pete's face grew red. How many times did he have to say it he wondered. He saw Edgar indicate he was to finish the oath. He shrugged and whispered to Edgar, "Okay, I'll go along wid youse one more time but that's it as far as I'm concerned." His voice got louder with each word. "Drop the ball."

As soon as he spoke the final words the stillness that had settled over the Clearing was broken by what sounded like the snap of something be released. Pete looked up to see what had caused the noise and froze when he saw the words, Ben Hog with a gash that covered what could be an kn or hn getting bigger as the Sphere covered the distance from the tree limb to him at an amazing speed.

"Ah boss you…" Was all Stubs got out before the sphere struck Pete on the top of the head and sent him tumbling to the ground.

Several in the crowd chased after the bouncing sphere, eventually caught up with it, rolled it back to the Committee meeting room and carefully placed it on its special stand in the corner.

The two lines of Community members gradually formed a circle around Pete who lay on the ground with Stubs crouched beside him calling his name and asking him to tell him how many paws he was holding up.

Edna pushed her way past the crowd that circled Pete and Stubs.

"Snnokems be careful, he could wake up at any moment." Edgar tried to prevent her from entering the circle.

She gave him a look that said, "One side or a leg off."

She moved closer to the prone figure and studied Pete's face. "Okay, which of you bozo's took my mother's antique seed collection?"

Edgar put his arm around her shoulder and made an attempt to move her to a safer place. "My little Brussels sprout, your upset about getting thrown out of our nest and…" He stopped and, judging from the look she gave him, realized he would have been better off if he'd stopped right after he said, "Brussels sprout."

Edgar's mouth continued to move but no sound came out.

"Lady, you'se is making one huge mistake here we don't know nothen about no seed collection." Stubs stood and towered over Edna.

She pushed by him and said, "Out of my way you nincompoop, I'm talking to him." She pointed at Pete.

Pete was groggy but gradually returning to normal. "Give her de collection Stubs," he mumbled, "then we's getten outta here." He paused a moment and looked at Edna. "That is, if it's okay wid youse."

Edna stared at him for a moment then turned and followed Stubs to the meeting room.

After she had received the antique seed collection she looked at the two intruders and said, "I think it's time for you to go." She pointed to the tall trees beyond Seed Man's yard and watched them leave through the small space that opened in the circle formed by the Community members.

Edgar started to say perhaps she'd gone a bit too far in talking to them like that but stopped when he heard her say to the departing figures, "And I don't want to see either of you around here again!"

The motion detector on the light by the kitchen door of Seed Man's house came on and Pete and Stubs momentarily froze, blinded by the light flooding the yard. They bumped into each other once and managed to stagger to the edge of the yard just as Seed Man came to the kitchen window to see what had caused the light to come on.

"Peach blossom, don't you think that's a little strong I mean shouldn't," he glanced in her direction and saw the look on her face. "I see, yes of course, that's exactly how I feel." He shouted at the backs of the two fleeing bullies who were well beyond any chance of hearing him, "We don't want to see the likes of you two again."

The Community members cheered and laughed thinking they would never have to worry about Pete O'Malley and Stubs showing up in the middle of the night and throwing them out of their nests again.

"Edgar, since we're all in our robes and everything, do you think we ought to go ahead and induct the new member into the Society?" Darin crossed the space between them and took his place next to Edgar.

"But we haven't had *the Night of Important Questions*. We haven't had the annual Society of Ben Hog dinner and lengthy discussion about the candidates. We haven't made them anxiously wait for us to…"

"There's only one candidate this year Edgar." Darin spoke quietly so those close by couldn't hear.

"Only one?" Edgar searched his memory but couldn't come up with who the lone candidate could be. "We discussed so many, remind me of who that candidate is."

"Roscoe," Darin gave a nod in Roscoe's direction.

"I see. I see." Edgar rubbed his chin and tried to think if there was some hidden rule in the Society by laws that would prevent them from eliminating *the Night of Important Questions*.

"He saved the Community honey bear, what's your problem?" Edna stood close to him and gave him a nudge with her elbow.

"But my precious milk toast it is a highly unusual practice. Why what if every…" Edgar flinched as Edna gave him another shot to the rib cage suggesting he should get on with it. "Roscoe, step forward. The rest of you form two lines. Jeffrey, get that button at the top of your robe taken care of."

Quickly the Society members found their places and made sure their official robes were buttoned and hanging properly.

Roscoe took his place opposite Edgar at the end of the two lines.

"Unless anyone objects, we will begin the installation of Ros…" Edgar watched in surprise as Roscoe raised his paw.

"Did you have a question Roscoe? It's highly unusual for the candidate to object to his own installation."

"Would it be possible to include four others without whom we would still be living under the fear of the return of Pete and Stubs, sir?"

"Four you say? Without whom…" Having one candidate admitted to the Society under these circumstances was pushing it for Edgar, suddenly the number had jumped to five.

"Who are the candidates you have in mind?" Darin spoke in the absence of a response from Edgar who, at the moment, had one paw against his forehead and was starring at the ground.

"Marvin and Jules were part of the team that helped put the plan together and did much of the leg work to make it happen." Roscoe was going to continue but the two lines came together and began discussing the inclusion of the two new names.

After a few minutes all the paws of the Society members were raised. Darin faced Roscoe. "Sure, that's okay with us. But you said four, that's just two."

"Sparky was the one who rigged up the device that dropped the Sphere on Pete. And, don't forget the role he played in getting Seed Man's garage door to open." Roscoe knew he was pushing it but Sparky was too valuable to the Community to be left off the list.

Darin looked at the Society members and they nodded yes. "Sparkys in. How about the last one?"

"I believe I speak for the three other candidates when I say that unless this person is included, we will withdraw our names from the official candidates list." Roscoe said it with such feeling no one in the Society took it as a threat, although none of them could imagine who the other candidate could be. They whispered among themselves possible names but would instantly dismiss them as either being too young or not a contributing member of the Community.

It wasn't long before everyone was looking at Roscoe, waiting for the announcement of the candidates name.

"Edna!" When Roscoe said her name it brought a gasp from Edgar; he looked like someone had stepped on his toe.

"But, she's a, a female. There have never been females in the Society. Why they could never learn the complicated handshake and the hundreds of rules that are necessary to memorize." Edgar's speech slowed as he looked behind the lines of the Society members and saw the faces of their wives and daughters standing behind them. They all seemed to be saying, "You've got to be kidding?"

Darin leaned close to Edgar and whispered, "Actually, Edgar, there's nothing in the rules that says a female can't be a member."

The look on Edgar's face said it all. "But what about the *Sacred Night of Bowling? Or, the Night of the Big Banquet* that comes right before the *Night of Important Questions*? Or how about *the Night of the Guys Getting Together In the Woods To Tell Funny Stories*?" He saw his last place to escape from Edna for a few hours slipping away. Edna? A member? He thought to himself.

The other society members felt the nudges and jabs from their wives standing behind them. One by one they raised their paws indicating that Edna should be included.

After the cheering that followed the vote lines formed again and the five candidates marched towards Edgar. Marvin and

Jules walked together behind Roscoe and Sparky with Edna proudly leading the way.

They stood quietly as Edgar solemnly read from the page in *The Society of Ben Hog,* titled, *Admitting New Members,* that outlined the ritual of induction.

Finally he came to the final admonition.

"And, most importantly, repeat after me, I Will Not Drop the Ball."

They repeated the phrase together but Edna added, "Unless someone that's disturbing the Community happens to be standing under it."

The crowd around her laughed and applauded her comment.

Edgar gave a half smile and knew in his heart of hearts the meetings of the Society he so dearly loved to attend would never be the same.